About the Author

Kate Grey is a dreamer, reader, and writer of all things romance. She lives in Florida with her husband, three children, and cocker spaniel. If she isn't home writing, she can more than likely be found at Disney World. She takes a minimum of three books on vacation and is always on the lookout for small or used bookstores. She hopes to create characters that readers can connect with and will be thinking about long after the final chapter.

Stronger Together

Kate Grey

Stronger Together

Olympia Publishers
London

www.olympiapublishers.com
OLYMPIA PAPERBACK EDITION

Copyright © Kate Grey 2023

The right of Kate Grey to be identified as author of
this work has been asserted in accordance with sections 77 and 78 of
the Copyright, Designs and Patents Act 1988.

All Rights Reserved

No reproduction, copy or transmission of this publication
may be made without written permission.
No paragraph of this publication may be reproduced,
copied or transmitted save with the written permission of the publisher,
or in accordance with the provisions
of the Copyright Act 1956 (as amended).

Any person who commits any unauthorised act in relation to
this publication may be liable to criminal
prosecution and civil claims for damage.

A CIP catalogue record for this title is
available from the British Library.

ISBN: 978-1-80439-192-1

This is a work of fiction.
Names, characters, places and incidents originate from the writer's
imagination. Any resemblance to actual persons, living or dead, is
purely coincidental.

First Published in 2023

Olympia Publishers
Tallis House
2 Tallis Street
London
EC4Y 0AB

Printed in Great Britain

Dedication

For my husband, Jonathan – I am the writer and mother I always dreamed of being, thanks to you. I love you always.

Acknowledgements

I would like to thank my parents for always supporting my love for books and reading. I would like to thank my mom for pushing me the last several years to start writing. I want to thank my children, Lilah, Jonah, and Elodie for being my inspiration and motivation to finally chase after my dream. Lastly, I want to thank my husband for encouraging me to take the time to complete this novel, start the next one, and for believing in me even when I didn't believe in myself.

Chapter 1

The rain is pitter-pattering on my window. I can't sleep so I watch as the raindrops blaze a trail running down the panes. It has been raining for the last five hours and I can hear it beating on the roof. Normally the sound would help me drift off to sleep and I could feel my body relax but not after the events of tonight. I don't think that anything will help me sleep after what I saw.

    I started having visions about five months ago. Visions that I had interpreted into being just bad dreams but then one of them came true. The image of Grace wrapped around a tree, her shiny silver Honda Accord mutilated, haunts me every time I close my eyes. They raced her to the hospital, but I already know that she isn't going to make it and my heart is aching. My best friend since preschool will be gone before daybreak and there isn't anything that I can do to save her.

    I can't tell a soul that I saw this coming. I just know that they will think I am crazy, driven mad by the loss of my best friend. My dad is barely keeping it together these days, so I know that he isn't an option. And as for my mom… nobody has seen her in three years. She dropped me off for my first day of high school and wasn't seen again. All I got was a lousy note left on my bed: "One day you will understand". The only thing I understand is that she was a selfish and heartless person that left her only daughter alone during the least trivial part of her life. However, I would do anything to be able to have her caress my head and calm me down like she had done since I was a little girl.

Not able to wrestle the pain any more, I slide on my boots and jacket and head for the front door. Thankfully my dad is a heavy sleeper and won't hear my steps on the creaky front porch. I just need to take a walk and clear my head. I can't sit around and wait for the phone call that she is gone. I tuck my cell in my back pocket, a habit my dad hates after I have broken multiple screens by sitting on them, and slide open the deadbolt. I grab my keys and lock it back into place.

I start strolling down the sidewalk illuminated by the orange glow of the streetlamps. The rain is still drizzling down and starting to soak through my navy-blue sweatpants but I can't feel the cold. I just feel empty and alone with only my dark thoughts to keep me company. I wander to the park that is only a few blocks away. The old swing set with the basketball and tennis courts bring back memories of Grace and I as kids. She always wanted to play and pretend we were princesses, but I wanted to pretend to be Jedi Knights, so we compromised and would be both. I would be waving around my light saber while she wore her crown. We were total opposites, but we were also as close as two friends could get, more like sisters.

As the memories rush back to me, I can taste the salt of my tears reaching my trembling lips. I didn't even realize I was crying due to the rain coating my face. Suddenly I am pulled out of my thoughts by the sound of the gate creaking open. I look up and there is a tall slim figure in a hoodie heading into the park. I stop moving the swing I have been sitting on and go still hoping that I haven't been seen. Who would possibly be out here at this time? One a.m. isn't generally a time that people come out to the parks unless they are up to no good. Or, like me, they are just trying to sort out their thoughts. I just knew I didn't want to find out which category this hooded figure fell into. I watch as it makes its way to a pavilion about fifty yards from where I am sitting. The only sound is the rain falling down around us and I am trying to figure out how I am going to make it out of the park unnoticed. I don't generally have to worry about things like this in my town but this wasn't someone I recognized, especially since I couldn't see their face. The figure climbs up on top of the picnic table back turned toward me and puts their head in their hands. I am going to assume that tonight we are both battling inner demons.

Suddenly I am startled as my phone starts ringing and I fumble to pull it out of my back pocket. I am trying to silence it but I accidentally hit the volume up button. My phone is ringing at full volume, "Ice Ice Baby" blasting into the silent night, and all hopes of going unnoticed have dissolved as I fight to quiet the noise. I finally grab hold of the phone to see my dad's smiling face on my screen. When I look up to where the figure was sitting, it is gone.

"Hello?"

"Gemma! Honey, where are you?" My dad's voice is frantic and rushed. Suddenly I feel a stab of guilt for leaving. He was already worried about Grace and here he was worried about me too.

"I'm just sitting at the park, Dad. I'm so sorry. I just needed some fresh air."

"Oh, sweetie, don't be sorry. I know tonight has been really rough on you. Want me to come get you? We need to talk." I felt like a rock had just sunk in my stomach. I knew the phone call had come. But the call hadn't gone directly to me, instead, my dad had received it. Mrs. Jennings probably assumed that he would be the best person to break any news to me.

"No, Dad, that's okay. I can walk. It's helping me clear my

head. I'll be right there." I hung up the phone, took a deep breath, and looked into the darkness around me. I hadn't even realized the rain had stopped, leaving cooler weather behind. A slight breeze touched my face as I exhaled the breath I didn't realize I was holding. I got to my feet, but when I looked up, the hooded figure was standing in front of me. I felt a chill run down my spine, as we locked eyes, illuminated by the moon that finally decided to appear from behind the rain clouds.

"Are you Gemma Jacobs?" The figure spoke with a voice like silk. He stood five inches above me with what appeared to be ashy blonde hair soaked to his forehead and blue eyes that felt like they were blazing through me. I was speechless. How did this stranger know who I was?

"Yeah... how did you know? Who are you?" I was finally able to stammer out. I felt the need to run through the gate and not look back, but I was paralyzed with both fear and curiosity. What did this boy want with me?

"None of that is important. You will have your answers in time. But right now, I have been sent with a warning." The chill intensified and I felt like all the oxygen on Earth had been sucked out of the atmosphere and all I could do was stare back.

"A... a uhh... a warning?" I let out a small nervous laugh. "What kind of warning? Like from the mob or something? What the hell is going on?" His face remained impassive as my mind raced. This can't be happening. Not tonight when I am already dealing with enough. There is no way.

"They know what you are. What you are capable of. They have been watching you and your visions but tonight... tonight one of them came to fruition. You are in great danger. Watch your back. Don't let your guard down." This can't be real. As I stared into his eyes, they seemed cold and detached. Almost like a robot as he delivered a warning that seemed like I was in a life or death situation. But I didn't have a clue who or what he was talking about and I still had no idea who he was.

"What is your name? Who are 'they'?"

"Goodbye, Gemma. Don't take this warning lightly. They have no mercy." With that, he pulled his hood further down and turned to leave. I tried to call after him, but he kept walking and didn't look back.

My mouth had gone dry and once he was out of sight, I ran. I ran all the way home as fast as my legs could carry me. I could hear my boots splashing in the puddles as I went, and I didn't care to look around and see if I had been followed. I reached my driveway and bounded up the front porch straight into the front door. As soon as I was inside, I locked the deadbolt and slid the chain on the door before sliding down the door to sit on the floor. My heart rate was racing, and I couldn't catch my breath. What had just happened? I have to be dreaming.

I heard footsteps coming from the kitchen and looked up to see my dad holding a steaming mug of tea. The corners of his mouth were drawn, his eyes were misty, and his hands were trembling. For the first time, I noticed how gray his hair had become and the stress lines on his forehead. I felt for him having to be the one to always break bad news to me. He was the one that picked me up from school on my first day to tell me that my mom had packed up and left. He was the one that told me when I was seven that my grandma Gertie had gone to heaven. And now he was the one that was about to deliver the blow that my best friend wasn't going to ever open her eyes again. "I'm glad you are home, peanut. I got some news that I didn't want to deliver over the phone." Hearing him use the nickname he had called me from the minute he found out my mom was pregnant made me feel warm and sad at the same time. I slowly stood up as he set down the mug on the table in the hallway. He outstretched his arms and I ran into them, feeling the tears spring to my eyes again. He wrapped them around me holding tight as I felt my body shaking against him.

"Grace is gone, isn't she, Dad? Gracie didn't make it. My best friend is dead, right?"

"Shh. Gemma. Everything is going to be okay. Shhhhh." I felt his hand stroking my hair as I listened to his heartbeat, trying to calm myself down. The feel of his old worn-out t-shirt rubbing against my cheek makes me feel like a kid again, if only these problems were as miniscule as my barbie's head popping off.

"Mrs. Jennings called. Grace had suffered some major head trauma and internal bleeding. They weren't able to save her. I am so sorry, peanut. I know she was your best friend. She also wanted me to tell you that she is so grateful that you were on scene to hold Grace's hand while waiting for the ambulance. That couldn't have been easy, but I am so proud of you and I know Grace was at peace with you beside her." My dad's voice is barely above a whisper. My sobs are now the only sound in the house.

Grace had been driving in front of me. We were heading home from a movie, but we didn't carpool because she was going to her boyfriend's house afterwards. He lived just a few miles from me. As we were going around a corner, one we had driven hundreds of times together, she lost control on the wet streets and ended up colliding with a tree. I pulled off to the side and for a second I couldn't will my feet to move because it was everything I had seen: the way the car went airborne, the sound of the tires sliding on the pavement, and the crunch of the metal on impact. Suddenly, my instincts kicked in and I was running toward her car to find her unconscious, dialing 911 as I went. I knew better than to try moving her so I climbed through the passenger side window and held her hand trying to talk to her until help had arrived.

The police called my dad and he drove me home while the ambulance took Grace to the hospital. That was around nine p.m. Here we are at almost two a.m. and she is gone. The last memory I have of her talking to me was as we climbed into our cars parked right next to each other and she said, "See? No matter what boyfriends come and go, I will always make time for my best friend. Love you, Gem." And with that she blew me a kiss, climbed into her car, started the engine, and off she went.

After finishing the tea my dad had made for me, I shook off my wet boots to head up stairs. My dad tucked me in like he did when I was a little girl, securing the blankets around my form like I am some sort of burrito. He kissed my forehead and turned out the light. I didn't dare tell him about my incident in the park.

I tried to shake the warning from my head. Could have all been some sort of hoax, right? But how would that guy know my name, about my visions, and what could they all possibly mean? I realized that my dad had made the sleepy time tea as my eyelids grew heavy and I surrendered to the darkness hoping that I could have a dreamless night.

I was standing in a hallway with the sound of the fluorescent lights buzzing overhead. The walls were peeling a sea foam shade of green and the tile looked like it belonged in my school cafeteria. I couldn't tell where I was. It wasn't anywhere I had been before and that I was sure of. I could feel the hair on the back of my neck stand up as I walked toward two voices, one that I know I had heard before. As I got closer, I realized it was the voice of the man in the park. He was talking in a hushed tone and he sounded like he was pleading. I came around a corner and entered into a room that appeared to be an old hospital. It reminded me of the ones in the history books with the wrought iron bed frames, small mattresses, and a few of them lined up in a room with the standup curtains that you could position around the beds for privacy. I paused but soon realized that nobody could see me. I wasn't really here.

I had been right about the blonde hair and the blue eyes. He was wearing a solid white t-shirt and jeans now and I could see the toned muscles in his arms. I also couldn't help but notice that the muscle in his jaw was locked, he was tense, and I have a feeling I had walked into a conversation that wasn't going his way. The person opposite of him was a woman; middle aged, long blonde hair that was almost white touched her lower back. She was standing in front of him with her arms crossed and piercing blue eyes, ones that looked just like his, were trained on him.

"You don't have to be the knight in shining armor here! The girl doesn't need your protection! There are many others that will step in and gladly keep an eye on her. With her lineage, any one of us would be willing to help if necessary. However, I just don't see the need for it at this point. I worry that if the SGP is onto her that you'll get caught in the line of fire. Please just keep your distance on this one."

"You don't understand!" He rose to his feet in defiance as his arms flailed around to help make his point. "She is clueless. I don't think she knows a thing about her lineage or what is happening to her. You have to let me protect her." I waited for the woman to respond and I was almost certain that they were talking about me. I saw her take a deep breath in and hang her head, arms crossed, and she looked resigned.

"Luca. Please be careful. You know better than anyone what SGP is capable of. They will stop at nothing. I'd never forgive myself if I let you do this and something happens to you." Her eyes suddenly looked tired and she looked a little older than I had anticipated. Luca, now that I knew what his name was, walked over and wrapped his arms around her shoulders. She came up to his chin and they embraced. "Don't worry, Mom," he said gently. "I promise I will be careful. Thank you."

Feeling as though I had just watched a private moment, I opened my eyes. I tried to shake away the sleep and focus enough to make sense of what I had just witnessed. Was it a dream? It couldn't have been a vision because it was a conversation taking place without me. The vision I had that came true, I had watched happen with my very own eyes. So what was this?

I looked at my phone. 8.42 a.m. on a Saturday. I raked my hands down my face, pulled my auburn hair into a ponytail, grabbed my clothes, and headed for the bathroom. I think what I need most right now is to wash the last twelve hours off of me. Too much has happened that I can't even process. Hopefully, a warm shower will help clear my mind.

I climbed into my red Toyota Tacoma, a gift from my dad on my sixteenth birthday, and started toward Grace's house. Mrs. Jennings, or Marilyn as she has asked me countless times to call her, was like a second mom to me. But since my own mom had left, she was the only mother figure I had any more. My eyes scanned down Acreage Way as I left. The majority of the houses here were two story and sat on a large piece of property with an immaculate yard. It wasn't the landscaping that I was admiring though. I was looking for the hooded man, Luca. If that was even really his name. Everything here looked exactly as it had the day before. It was a warm July afternoon and the only thing that was missing was Grace.

I pulled into her driveway shortly before noon with a coffee from Starbucks, her mom's favorite. Before I could climb out of the car, Marilyn had appeared in the doorway wearing a varsity cheerleader shirt of Grace's and her hair pulled back. It looked like she had aged five years overnight but as I approached, she grabbed me and pulled me in for a hug. I didn't handle people crying very well but I rubbed her back and absorbed her sobs. "She loved you so much, dear. You have no idea how much it means to a parent to know their child had a friend like you in their life."

I felt the knot in my throat and I couldn't swallow past it. Thankfully, Grace's dad came up behind her and took her arms from around me and led her in the house. I know he was staying strong for her and gave me an apologetic look as if to say sorry for his sorrow filled wife. I followed them in the big oak front door. As I looked around the house that was like a second home to me since I was five, I felt like a stranger. The wood floors that I had run across so many times, the living room that we turned into a dance floor to songs by One Direction and Taylor Swift, the kitchen where we had shared so many Friday Night Sleepover pizzas all seemed foreign without her laugher and light filling each room. I looked over the pale blue walls that made me think of sea mist with their white frames scattered about. Pictures of Grace were everywhere because, like me, she was an only child and the light of their life. I knew I couldn't stay long because the emotional toll her parents were going through needed private mourning and this home felt like it was smothering me, a reminder of the life lost that I should have saved.

Mr. Jennings sat his wife on the couch and I took a seat

across from them on the loveseat. It took her a few minutes to compose herself as we sat in silence. Just the sound of her sniffling but she finally wiped her face and looked at me with eyes so sad, it broke my heart.

"Thank you for coming by, Gemma. I know you're hurting just as much as we are and thank you again for being with our little girl last night. We are so grateful she had you and didn't have to be afraid." Marilyn looks down at her hands and twists her soggy tissue into a twist before unraveling it and dabbing at her eyes. "You are still like a daughter to us so please, don't be a stranger. You are more than welcome to come over anytime. I think we will be needing your company now more than ever."

"Of course. You guys are my family too and I am always here. Please call me for anything, anytime." I didn't know what else to say. I know that, though she tried to replace the mother that left me, I could never replace the daughter she has lost.

"Once we get our bearings, I do want you to take a few things from her room. Things that I feel you should have and perhaps a few tokens to remember her by. That is what she would have wanted." She looks down again and I can see her body rattling with the emotion threatening to break loose. So I decide it is time to wrap up.

I visited for a few more minutes while they shared that Grace would be cremated, just a memorial service where everyone was to wear her favorite color (yellow), and then I was on my way. As I walked down the drive back to my truck, I turned and took in the house again. Even the house looked like it was mourning and knew that the walls would never hear her laughter, the stairs would never know the feeling of her children's feet running up and down them, and the bedroom that she once had would never be inhabited again.

As I headed home, I passed by the same park that I had been to only hours earlier and saw kids playing on the swings, teenagers a few years younger than me were playing basketball, and off to the side at one of the pavilions, the same one as the day before, was Luca, wearing the same white shirt and jeans that I remembered from my dream last night... or whatever that was. I pulled into the parking lot and got out.

He could be a psychopath and I could end up on *Dateline* as the girl that went missing in the park. Nobody suspected a thing as the two strode out of the park together. She was such a nice girl, quiet, and didn't have many friends. He was mysterious and nobody knew who he was. I could see it already as they interviewed my dad, the kids at the park, and Mr. and Mrs. Jennings since they were the last people to speak to me. OR he could be someone that wants to protect me and he owes me some explanations. Either way, I felt that it was worth the risk. What did I have to lose anyway?

I passed through the same gate but he didn't look up, not seeming to notice that I had entered. All the noise around us drowned out my steps. The trees hung over the sidewalk providing shade, a cool breeze still lingered from the rain, and the sun was bright without a cloud in the sky. I walked up behind him and before I could lose my courage I decided I was just going to spit everything out, lay it all out on the table, and hopefully get to the bottom of things.

"You're Luca, aren't you? The guy that was in the park with me last night?" He turned to face me with surprise and wonder in his eyes. My guess was he had to be about nineteen years old. Being this close to him, merely a few feet away, I noticed that he had a few freckles across the bridge of his nose. His upper lip upturned slightly making them appear to be full. He had a small scar above his left eyebrow and very prominent cheekbones. His blonde hair just grazed the top of his forehead and was shaven down on the sides. He looked almost unrealistically... handsome.

"How'd you know my name?" His eyes crinkled in the corners as he squinted at me in confusion. It seemed that unlike last night, I now had the upper hand.

"Listen. I don't know who you are or what you want with me. But I need to know... how did you know about my vision?" I noticed that I was fidgeting with my hands and quickly dropped them down to my sides. Confidence is key. I learned that in my speech class last year. Focus.

"You'll get your answers but here isn't the time and place. They could be watching us and any information we share with one another needs to be done confidentially. Alone." As Luca spoke, I couldn't help but watch his mouth. I realize that I am staring at his pouty bottom lip.

"If you think I will be alone with someone who can't even answer a few questions, you're insane. I am not going to be another *20/20* Friday night special. So either you spill or I walk." There you go. Stick it to him. If Grace could see me now, she would be so proud of me. However, a smirk played at the corners of his mouth as if he thought this was some sort of joke. He was actually mocking me.

"You think that your disappearance would be worthy of a *20/20* special?" He chuckled slightly. "There are roughly two thousand kids that get abducted each year. Some sold into trafficking, some murdered, and some taken by their own family members never to be seen again and they don't all get TV time. Or is it because you live in an upper middle-class neighborhood that makes you newsworthy?" He smirked and shook his head before standing. "You know what. I came here to try giving you the answers you seek. On second thoughts though, you don't seem like the type that I generally go out of my way for. Good luck."

I was completely dumbfounded. Nobody had ever spoken to me like that and this guy was a complete stranger. He didn't know me from the next eighteen-year-old girl passing him on the streets. He was arrogant and walking away. Unfortunately for me, after last night, I needed answers.

"Wait!" I sighed as he turned around, crossing his arms, and giving me a gloating look. "You're right. I do need answers. Like I want to know what the hell the SGP is and what they would want with me." As soon as the words left my mouth, I knew it hadn't been a good idea.

He covered the distance between us in three quick strides and was right in my face. The gloating turned to fear as he peered into my eyes. His voice came out in a whisper. "Don't ever say that out loud. You shouldn't even know what that is. HOW do you know what that is? Actually. Don't answer that." He grabbed my wrist and we were walking. My curiosity got the best of me so I didn't fight him. I did look around to see if anybody had witnessed our encounter or was looking at us with suspicions, but nobody even seemed to notice that we were there.

We arrived at a shiny four door Audi. Black and sleek. The guy that just went off on me about my upper middle-class neighborhood drives an Audi? Repulsive. He opened the passenger door and gestured for me to get in before shutting the door and joining me.

"How do you know about them? Who else has been in touch with you? I need to know." He was frantic and talking fast. His hands were shaking and I couldn't tell if he was angry or scared.

Either way, I felt surprisingly at ease in the car beside him like I was safe and nothing could happen to me.

"I dreamt about it last night. About you and I think your mom. You mentioned them and I think you were discussing me." My voice was barely a whisper, I was fidgeting with my hands again, and I looked up to find his cool blue eyes on me.

"What do you mean that you dreamt about me?" His voice was now calm and relaxed as if this minor detail was more important than what we were really here to discuss. I blushed, suddenly embarrassed that I was so forthcoming with information like that.

"We were in what appeared to be an old abandoned hospital. I think you were in a room talking with your mom about a girl that needed protecting. Something about her lineage and being naïve to whatever it is that is going on. Were you asking to protect me?" He exhaled, clearly bewildered. I got a sudden chill. It wasn't a dream. It was another vision because now he can't even bring himself to look at me.

"I was. That conversation took place after I left the park last night. My mom doesn't seem to agree with me which I am guessing you saw? You just seem new to all of this. Did you see or hear anything else?" Luca looks at me puzzled.

"That was really it. Just that you were wanting to protect me and she agreed but was worried about the SGP because she said you of all people knew what they were capable of." He looked away, scanning the parking lot around us, the park, and checked the rearview mirror. It was like he was antsy and worried that he was being followed. Or worse, that I was being followed. We sat in silence for a few minutes while it seemed he was trying to get his thoughts together. He opened his mouth a few times to talk before shutting it like he was struggling to find the words to say.

"You had a vision. You watched your friend die in that car accident yesterday. Now you're telling me that you were dreaming of an event that was happening in that exact moment without trying to. I think your abilities reach far beyond what we had originally anticipated." He scratched his chin in thought.

"Who is we? What are you apart of?"

"We are The Gifted Alliance. We are a group of individuals that live normal lives but with special talents. We formed The Alliance after the SGP tried to recruit us into their department. It stands for Supernatural Government Protection. It sounded tempting. They said they would keep us safe as long as we offered our services for the 'greater good' in return. Only after some people joined, we learned that it isn't used for helping catch terrorists or solve world hunger. Their abilities are used against our own people. To torture them, track down other innocent people with abilities, con citizens out of their fortunes, and much worse. We are being used against our own people. Once they catch wind of your visions, they'll be after you too."

"Wait... there are more like me? Many more? I mean, I only had the one vision that came to fruition and, as of last night, the one dream. How could that really mean anything to anyone?" I heard my heart racing in my ears, the blood pumping through my veins, and I was covered in goosebumps. All my life I have been ordinary. I was a runner on the track team, played the saxophone in the marching band, took a few AP classes, but everything else about me was ordinary. I was ordinary from the 5'6" that I measured in at, to the Converse that I sat here in, and I had never even had a boyfriend. There was nothing that was "gifted" or "supernatural" about me.

"I have extremely heightened senses. I can hear a conversation from over a mile away. I can see equally as far. I am able to pick and choose when I use them so I can live a normal life and not have to hear everything or see more than what is in front of me." I can imagine things must be pretty loud for Luca, especially if he didn't have the control."

"What about me? How did you know about my visions?"

"That would be because of my mom. She has the ability to detect when people have these 'talents' and once your friend's car wrecked, validating your vision, she knew it. So she sent me here to try and find you."

My head was spinning. I had too many questions but I couldn't formulate them. I needed time. This sounded like it was out of a movie and couldn't possibly be real life but how else could I explain the wreck? The dream? The fact that Luca knew where to find me and knew about it as well?

"I... I have to go. It is starting to get late and my dad will expect me for dinner." Before he could even utter another syllable, I got out of the car. He didn't try to stop me or make a move like he wanted to continue the conversation. As I started walking to my truck, I heard the silent pur of his engine as he left me in the parking lot, my head swimming with questions that I was afraid to get answers to.

I sat in the driveway and took in my house, the house that I had grown up in, the only home that I had ever known. From the way the light blue paint was starting to chip in places, the white shutters and front porch, the heavy door that I had walked through so many times. There was a gardenia bush on either side of the sidewalk before ascending the stairs that my dad had planted for my mom when I was little. They were her favorite flower and, even with her gone, he made sure they got fed, pruned, and watered regularly.

When she first left, I had to hold my nose from the car to the house so I wouldn't have to breathe them in. Their perfume scent reminded me of my mom and it was too painful. On days that I miss her, or on days like today where I just feel lost, I pause and inhale as deep as I can. As the scent floods my body, so does the warmth of her memory. As time goes on, the pain lessens and I am able to think about her without falling apart.

When people hear that my mom left, they always assume that she must've been a bad parent. I can understand how that would be their first thought seeing as how she did walk out on her only child without any reason or warning but she was actually a very loving and attentive mother. She ran the school bake sale every year since I was in kindergarten. She braided my hair every which way in the mornings before school. I received notes in my lunchbox a minimum of twice a week, and every birthday, she decorated my room while I slept and baked me my favorite cake for breakfast. She kissed all scraped knees and watched my favorite Disney movies on replay, even giving me Princess Leia buns when I went through a phase in seventh grade. She was everything I had ever wanted to be.

I walk up the sidewalk to my front door, pausing at the gardenias for a few deep breaths, and raise my eyes to the sky. "I don't know where you are, Mom, but I could really use you right now. I wish you were here to say goodbye to Grace with me. I just wish I knew you were okay." I look back down to the sidewalk and see where my dad had me put my hands into the cement a few summers back. My name is like chicken scratch, carved in using a stick.

I walk inside and head toward the kitchen. My dad has left a note on the counter: "Went to meet with clients. There is leftover lasagna in the fridge. Love ya." Dad was one of the top real estate agents in town so he often was out on the weekends showing houses to potential clients.

I heat up a plate and start for the stairs. As I walk by the front door, I double check that it is locked and when I peek out the small window, I catch a glimpse of a black Audi driving by. In spite of myself, I can feel my stomach flutter as I take the steps two at a time.

Chapter 2

It was Monday morning and I had just slid on the only yellow garment I owned: a yellow sundress that tied on the shoulders and would float in the breeze. I observed myself in the mirror. I had dark circles under my eyes that concealer wouldn't cover, I applied some lip gloss, smoothed down my hair, and gave myself one last onceover. I hadn't been sleeping very well. Between Grace and Luca, I felt disoriented and like I was barely functioning in this thick fog. The knock on my door startled me. "Uhh yeah? Come in."

My dad walked in wearing a pair of navy-blue dress pants, a yellow dress shirt, and a navy-blue tie with yellow daisies on it. Seeing him made me relax a little as he gave me a reassuring smile.

"Almost ready, peanut? We should get going. You look lovely." I smiled at him appreciatively. This man didn't ever get the thank you and credit he deserved. I grabbed my white sandals and slid them on my feet.

"Thank you, Dad, for umm… everything. Not just today and for going with me but just for… just for always being here for me. I don't say it enough." We didn't do this sappy love stuff so I could tell I caught him off guard as he shifted his weight from foot to foot. Then he closed the space between us and took me in for a bear hug.

"I will always be here, Gemma. I am never going anywhere. I promise you on everything and I will do whatever you need from me today. I am your guy." He pulled back and smiled that same reassuring smile but this time his eyes had gone a little misty and he excused himself. "I will meet you in the car when you're ready."

I heard him walk down the stairs and knew when he hit the third step from the bottom. It had started creaking a few years ago. He always teased that it was our own alarm system so he would know if I ever tried to sneak out. Once, Grace and I were sneaking down to the kitchen to get ice cream at midnight and as we went for the spoons, he flipped the kitchen light on. "Stair alarm," he had said. "But while we are all here, lets break out the toppings, girls. If you are going to sneak ice cream, at least do it right." Grace and I couldn't help but laugh. It was one of my favorite memories with her in my house.

I reached for my purse and cell phone finding that I had a text from an unknown number. It read, "BE CAREFUL TODAY. BE OBSERVANT OF YOUR SURROUNDINGS. DON'T GO ANYWHERE ALONE. – L." I know that the first thing that should have crossed my mind is fear, but really what crossed my mind was how did he get my number? There wasn't any time to think about that or anything else for that matter. Today was for Grace, Marilyn, and Mr. Jennings. They needed my undivided attention and I could worry about the rest later.

As my dad pulled us away from the house, I noticed a silver SUV pulled out behind us. I am sure it is my overactive imagination. I mean, this neighborhood had tons of cars coming and going. There wasn't any way that I could have them all memorized. However, the limo-like tint made me a little apprehensive. Who needed tint that dark unless they were doing something illegal or some sort of undercover government job? I made sure to monitor its movements as we drove the short distance to the church. It always managed to stay a few cars behind us but close enough that I always knew where it was.

"I know today is going to be rough. I have a closing after the memorial though so I will have to drop you off at home as soon as it's over or you can catch a ride with a friend if you'd like." He reaches over and pats me on the knee.

"Thanks, Dad. I'm okay with heading home afterwards. I don't think I will really be up for much else." As we pulled into the church, I watched as the silver SUV drove past the church. I felt myself relax without realizing how tight my chest felt. I knew I was overreacting. I slid out of my dad's white Volvo and saw that in the back of the parking lot, there was a black sleek Audi with the same limo tint as the SUV. I should have known that Luca was watching me.

I hadn't seen him since Saturday when I watched him drive away from my house but I knew that he was always around. I couldn't explain it but it was like I was the one with the heightened senses and I could feel him keeping a watchful eye on me from a distance. Seeing the car wiped all thoughts of the SUV from my mind. Nothing would happen on Luca's watch. Something about him made me feel like I can genuinely trust him, which really said a lot because I hadn't trusted anyone new since my mom left.

The service was nice. Just about everyone showed up in yellow as requested but the part that angered me was watching the people from school show up. Most of them didn't even know Grace. Though she was a cheerleader, she didn't hang out with them or run in the same circles they did. Nonetheless, they showed up to her memorial and cried like they had been the best of friends. It was like a big social gathering for them complete with selfies and I had to watch it all knowing that they were the last people Grace wanted here.

As her best friend, there were pictures of her and I all through the slideshow. There was a picture of us at Disney when my parents took us for my tenth birthday. She was standing on one side of Cinderella and I was on the other, wearing matching princess shirts. There was another picture of her and I at a Taylor Swift concert. The tickets were a gift from her parents for her thirteenth birthday. My favorite of them all though was a picture of our families together. There was Marilyn, Brad (that is her dad), my mom, my dad, Grace, and me all sitting in Times Square when they took us for our sixth-grade graduation. I had completely forgotten about the picture but it made me cry even harder seeing that two of the people in that photo were gone and the rest of us were changed forever.

They played a few of her favorite songs. People were allowed to share memories of her. I watched as her boyfriend, Zach, got up and talked about her. He was the only boyfriend she had ever had and they were together for a little over a year. He talked about the time that Grace tried to surprise him for his birthday and take him somewhere but had gotten lost. She refused to tell him where it was she was taking him but ended up having to cave when she asked him to look up the directions. We all chuckled because anyone who knew Grace also knew that she was horrible with directions. She grew up in this small town but still hadn't figured out how to get around. She often asked, "Is that toward the Starbucks or away from it?" The Starbucks was the center for all directions.

I decided to get up and deliver a speech. It was hard to keep my emotions in check but I gathered up the strength to walk up to the podium. I felt that, after so many years of friendship, I owed it to her and her parents.

"Grace and I were more than best friends. She was my sister too. We had big plans to build houses next door to each other once we got married, raise our kids so they could grow up and be best friends, and planned to open a dog daycare. Grace loved all things full of life whether it was people, animals, or even plants. She claimed to have a green thumb but she killed the rose bush I got her when she decided she wanted to start a nursery. We were supposed to attend Notre Dame together one day. She had big dreams and I am really going to miss hearing them. Grace never saw the bad in anyone and only ever looked for the good. She saw the best in me and made me want to be better. When my mom left—" Here I looked over at my dad to gauge his reaction. I hadn't considered how he would feel hearing this until this moment. I took a deep breath and continued. "When my mom left, she used to sneak out and climb in my room at night. Nobody knew that but I had a hard time sleeping alone and she would come lay in bed with me until I had fallen asleep before sneaking back out. That was the kind of friend she was. She would ride her bike a few miles just so I wasn't alone. Grace. I am going to miss your laugh, your hugs, and the future we were supposed to share as sisters. I love you."

Marilyn's sob escapes in the silence as I make my way down from the podium where dad is awaiting with arms wide open. He pulls me in and kisses the crown of my head. "Good job peanut", is all he says before we sit and listen to the pastor.

After the service, I went to hug her parents. Marilyn pulled me in holding me tight and whispered, "We always knew she was sneaking out to see you. But we knew you needed her and we knew that even if we tried to stop her, her love for you would trump whatever it was we had to say." I felt her wipe the tears from my eyes and she smiled at me. "Please come over anytime. You are my daughter too, Gemma. Nothing can change that." Then she handed me a little yellow urn. It was so small that it fit in the palm of my hand. Its size didn't matter to me because the gesture was the biggest one anyone had ever shown me. "She would have wanted you to have a little bit of her with you wherever you went. Please take care of the piece of her that is here." I was stunned to know that they had entrusted me with a little of what was left of their daughter.

"Thank you. I promise to cherish her and keep her close." I peered at this little urn and couldn't help but think this was all I had left of her.

I felt my dad's hand on my elbow as he said our goodbyes and guided me to the door. I had never felt so emotionally exhausted in my life. My mom may be gone but she wasn't dead. I felt that, if she was, someone would have found us and told us by now. There wasn't anything final about her absence but with Grace, all I had left were the memories and the ashes in this little urn.

We made our way through the crowd once we got out of the church. I looked up and saw Luca making his way toward us, eyes locked on me, and I knew something was wrong. I also couldn't help but notice the way the girls in the crowd watched him. It was like they had never seen a boy before as they marveled at his long strides. I could see Bridgett, the cheerleading captain, with her mouth open in awe. He stopped in front of me and plastered a huge fake smile on. I could tell it was forced and that he was extremely tense.

"Mr. Jacobs. Hello. My name is Luca Andrews and I am a friend of Gemma's." Luca extended his hand and I could tell he was trying very hard to make a good impression on my dad. "It is a pleasure to finally meet you, sir. Mind if I have a word with her?" My dad looked back and forth between us and was clearly confused. He knew all the people that I was friends with so I know he was racking his brain for a mention of a Luca. He could take all the time in the world searching for it but it would never come.

"Nice to meet you, Luca. And just how do you and Gemma know each other?" Luca paused, clearly not knowing me well enough to know how our connection could be plausible. He looked to me for help.

"Luca and I are in the marching band together. Yeah, he plays the triangle. It was the only instrument that Mr. Marcos would let him touch. He is really clumsy and horrible at reading music." I can see Luca out of the corner of my eye tuck his head down and stifle a laugh. So he does have a sense of humor? That is a relief because after the day I've had, I need to let loose a little bit.

"Interesting. I didn't know the band had a triangle. Well, Luca, I am sorry but we are in a bit of a hurry. I need to drop Gemma off at home so I can make it to an appointment. Take care." Before my dad could take another step, Luca stepped into our path.

"I can take her home, Mr. Jacobs. It would be my pleasure. That is, if Gemma is all right with it? I drive much better than I play instruments. I promise she will be safe." Now it was my turn to smirk and hold back the laughter threatening to spill out. I haven't laughed or smiled since leaving the movies three days earlier. I feel the tightness in my chest that I have been carrying around ease just a little. I feel like my lungs are at least filling with a little bit of air now.

"Yeah, Dad, it's fine. Luca can take me home. I was hoping

to stop for a coffee or something on the way home anyway."

"Okay, Gemma but please text me when you make it home safely. And, Luca, this is my little girl. She is all I have. No texting and driving and get her home safely." My dad glances over Luca one last time, committing every feature and article of clothing to detail. We are completely paranoid in this family.

"Yes sir. You have my word. You can trust me."

"I don't trust any boys when it comes to my daughter but I will take your word for it." Then we watched as my dad walked to his car and waited until he was out of earshot. I looked around at the people from school watching us. I know what they were thinking. What was someone like Luca, who looks like he just walked off of a runway in Milan, doing talking to someone like me, the poster child for goody two shoes.

"Listen. We will talk when we get to my car so, for now, just act natural and try not to look around too much." We walked in a comfortable silence to his car that he must've left on, he opened my door for me like before, and inconspicuously glanced around the parking lot before climbing in beside me.

"You were followed here today," Luca tells me as he buckles his own seatbelt.

"By a silver SUV?" I knew they looked suspicious.

"You noticed that? So you got my text message then."

"I did notice. I didn't expect anyone to find me so fast."

"They have their... reasons for being able to find you so quickly. Have you had any more visions or dreams?"

I shook my head. "Nothing besides what I have told you." He put the car in drive and we were off heading toward the Starbucks. He must've really taken me seriously when I said I wanted a coffee. I was just trying to buy us time but now it is all I can think about.

"Good. Keep me updated if anything changes. The car that followed you showed up a few hours before you left this morning. I have been sure to watch your house through the night. I was waiting for the sign that they were on to you but I don't think they suspect that you know anything." His eyes were shifty. I can't imagine what kind of training or life he had to have had that made him so aware. It was like he was used to watching his back twenty-four-seven.

"What did you mean when you said that they have their reasons for being able to find me so quickly?" I ask quizzically. I feel like I am lighting up on a radar or something.

"I would rather explain once we put some more space between us and them. The only reason I was able to get to you is because they left shortly after the service. They probably knew they couldn't get you alone with your dad present but that doesn't mean they aren't close by." We pulled into the drive-thru and he placed our orders, two caramel Frappuccinos, one with no whip cream, and a banana nut bread. Apparently, his sneaking around and tailing me had caused him to have quite the appetite.

We drove listening to some rock music that I didn't recognize but I watched as he absentmindedly drummed his fingers on the steering wheel to the beat. He was driving us away from town toward the lakes, I assumed for the privacy and not for the lack of cellphone service in the area. I was taking the scenery in. The tall trees and the way their shadows cast across the road. The bright sun without a cloud in the sky dousing everything in its light. I knew we were supposed to be secretive but I wished more than anything that I could roll the windows down and feel the breeze on my face and inhale the crisp scent of the air. Instead, I was surrounded by black leather and a dark window tint that allowed me to enjoy the view from the inside but almost made it seem like it was out of reach.

Almost as if he had read my thoughts, Luca rolled the windows down and I saw the corner of his mouth turn up with a smile of satisfaction as the wind blasted us and whipped my hair around. Despite the day that I was having, I couldn't help but laugh and throw a hand out the window. Then we were turning off the main road onto a small access road that led around the lake. He found us a secluded area where he parked the car under a tree.

As I step out of the car, I take in the beauty with awe. The way the light filters through the trees overhead and how it seems like I am in a whole different town or state or country. This little slice of heaven I didn't know existed. I am so entranced that I don't notice Luca has walked around the car and is now standing at my side.

"Mind if we do a little walking? I know you aren't exactly… dressed for the occasion but it isn't a difficult distance to cover." He was looking at my white strappy sandals with amusement.

"Uhh yeah, sure. I haven't been back this way before. Where are we exactly?"

"This is where I come to think. It is quiet here and nobody seems to know where that access road leads so I haven't ever bumped into anyone." I was glancing around when I felt his eyes were on me. I stared back for a few moments. "I know you have a lot of questions. SGP won't find us here so I will try to give you all the answers you're looking for. Let's get to the water first." He started walking but I could tell that he was taking smaller and slower strides than he was used to so I could keep up. He would catch himself getting a little far ahead and then he would pause until I had closed the gap. We were silent at first but then I realized how little I really knew about him.

"So tell me about yourself? I didn't even know your last name until about forty-five minutes ago." He glances over his shoulder uninterested.

"What do you want to know? I can assure you that I am not too interesting of a specimen."

"Well... how old are you?" I stumbled over a rock trying to mimic his footsteps and felt his hand jump out to steady me.

"Watch your step." He now sounds annoyed with me. "And I am nineteen." I was right. He was just a year older though he carries himself like he is much older than that.

"Where are you from?"

"Originally? From a little town called Cocoa Beach in Florida. Relocated to Cape James about four years ago." Four years ago? But I had never seen him before. Cape James was a small town, the kind where everyone knew everybody. You'd think that Luca would be a person that was hard to miss.

"What brought you here? Most people move TO Florida. Not away from it."

"North Carolina isn't so bad. But to answer your question, this is where our Alliance headquarters is. After my mom and dad divorced, she and I moved up here for a fresh start and to be closer to people that... understood who we were." I let this soak in. A headquarters? That meant there were more people like me and close by. Suddenly the world didn't seem so big and intimidating knowing that we weren't alone. "Here is my spot. Consider yourself lucky. I haven't shared it with anyone."

He was standing on a small hill that obscured my view of the lake. I walked up to stand next to him and gasped. I had seen Lake Anne hundreds, if not thousands, of times. But never had I seen it like this. The water stretched in both directions, disappearing around a bend to the left. The tall trees across from us stood like giants protecting the land. There was a slight breeze that ruffled the branches over head and the water lapped at the shore just below our feet. I couldn't see or hear a boat. There were no kids on a rope swing. No sight of another human being anywhere. It was peaceful, quiet, and completely undisturbed. It was like a private oasis that wrapped around you like a blanket of warmth and serenity.

"It is breathtaking. I haven't ever seen it like this. I can't believe I have been here my whole life and this feels like I have been let in on a secret the lake has been withholding from me." My cheeks were hurting from the grin stretching across my face. I descend the slope and feel the soft sand beneath my feet. I slide off my shoes and stick my toes in the water. I close my eyes to breathe it all in when I feel Luca join me.

"It is the perfect place to get the answers you've been seeking. Where do you want to start?" He puts his hands in his pockets and stares out over the water.

"In the dream, you mentioned my lineage. What was that about?" It was the biggest question that had been eating away at me but I felt that it was so wrong to ask it since it wasn't information that I was supposed to know.

"Diving right in I see?" Luca sighed and shook his head. "That is the one topic that I don't know a ton about. I do know that your mom was part of the Alliance at one time. She was the one that encouraged my mom to pick up and move us here. But we know she left a few years ago and she dropped off the map. Nobody has been able to find or contact her and I know my mom has tried. I never met her but I know that your mom had an exceptional gift and was a pretty important person to our headquarters." I felt like the world was standing still for the third time in four days. My mom? He knew something about my mom. Luca knew something about the woman I spent fifteen years with that I didn't even know.

"What was my mom's gift?" Luca looked at me in shock.

"You really don't know anything about it? At all?" I shook my head trying to keep my lip from trembling. "Your mom has the ability to make people see things that aren't there. It is some type of mind trick and everything feels real and seems real but it isn't. It is all in your head. Basically a hallucination. She is exactly the type of person that SGP would want to recruit to their side. Instead, she helped form the Alliance about twenty years ago. You have it in your blood."

"Oh God. Does my dad know? Is that why she left us? How could she keep something this... this BIG from me? Her own daughter!" I could feel my blood pressure rising and I couldn't catch my breath. Luca made a move to try to comfort me. "Please don't. I will be fine I just... I just need a minute to calm down. This is a big revelation!"

"I think your dad knew if it helps at all but he wouldn't have shared that information to protect your mom." That didn't help. It only made matters worse. So my dad, the guy that held my hand through the memorial just a few hours ago, that watched as I struggled with my mom's departure the day of homecoming, the day I got my license, on my sixteenth birthday when she wasn't there to sing happy birthday, he knew this and didn't share it with me?

"Change of subject. What happened with you and the SGP?"

Without a moment of hesitation, he replied, "Next question. No relevance."

"OH COME ON! That is totally a relevant question. How else will I know what I am supposed to be so afraid of?"

Luca appeared angry all of a sudden. His normally passive eyes looked like they were filled with rage. "Can't you just take my word for it? Isn't that enough for you? I am already out here risking my neck to protect you because nobody cared to share these details with you so can we not just focus on that?" He looked back toward the water but continued to clench and unclench his fists. His words stung. Nobody had cared enough to share with me and I was kept in complete darkness.

"You know what? You are absolutely right. Nobody has cared enough to talk about it with me. The one person who may have actually been able to guide me through this walked out on me. Does that make you happy to hear? So don't worry about risking your neck any longer. Just take me home." I turned to start the trek to the car, tears filling my eyes, and blurring my vision. As I tried to climb back up the small hill, my foot slipped but once again Luca's arms steadied me as I fell backwards.

"You are so clumsy. It is a wonder that you've made it this far." He was teasing me and all anger or malice from his voice had evaporated.

Once steady on my feet again I turned to face him. "Look. I'm sorry for my outburst. I don't like talking about my past or the experiences I had. Just trust me when I say that the SGP aren't people you want to meet or mess with. They are manipulative, deceitful, and destructive." He looked down but I could see the anger had been replaced by pain. "They are the reason my parents divorced so can we just leave it at that?"

"No need to apologize. It is just all a little overwhelming."

"I understand and I forgot to say it but I am really sorry about your friend. Still want to leave?" Did I want to leave? Not really. Was my dad going to start panicking? Yes.

"Yeah I think we should. It has been a long day and I don't want my dad to freak."

The ride home was quiet and uneventful. We just listened to music the whole way but as we got closer to town, the windows went up and his eyes started scanning our surroundings. I was looking for the silver SUV too but it seemed to have given up for the day. We pulled into my neighborhood and Luca stopped at the end of my driveway. I opened the door to climb out and heard him clear his voice. "Uhh sorry. I think it is best that your dad not know what I drive for now. I don't want him to be suspicious since I patrol the neighborhood and sit down the block sometimes." Duh. I hadn't even thought of that.

"No this makes total sense. Thanks for the ride and for the information. I appreciate it. See ya around." I strolled up to the door and heard the Audi pulling away. I noticed that my dad wasn't home yet. It was only a little after four p.m. so that wasn't highly unusual for him. Before I unlocked the door I remembered that he wanted me to text him that I made it. I checked in and then headed inside.

Once crossing over the threshold into the house, I began to feel uneasy. Something was off. Something didn't feel right. Someone had either been here or was here now. There was almost like an electric current in the air. I could feel it all around me as I scanned the living room to my left, the hallway straight ahead leading to the kitchen, the staircase to my right, but I didn't see anything out of place. The door had been locked when I came in but I couldn't put my finger on it.

"Dad?" I called out. Maybe he had decided to park his car in the garage. It wasn't like he hadn't before but he normally only did that when it was raining outside. There wasn't a response and, looking on the wall to the left of the front door, his keys weren't hanging on the hook. I had a bad feeling about this and turned to go when someone called out to me.

"Miss Jacobs. How nice of you to finally join us. A shame you kept us waiting."

Chapter 3

My blood ran cold. Goosebumps broke out all over my body. I was suddenly numb from head to toe. My mouth was dry. My brain didn't know if it needed to kick in the fight or flight mode.

"Who are you?" There were two perpetrators standing in my foyer. The one talking to me was a tall, thin man dressed in black pants and a black polo with black shoes. He had to stand at least a foot taller than me. He was accompanied by a shorter, muscular man. He had his brown hair in a buzz cut, sunglasses on, with jeans and a tight black shirt that showed off how many hours he spent in the gym. Both were intimidating and I was very afraid.

"Now Gemma. Let's not play games. You know exactly who we are and why we are here. We know you've been keeping company with Luca. He is slick but not slick enough. So why don't we just cut to the chase, shall we?" He gestured toward the living room, MY LIVING ROOM, inviting me to sit down on the couch as if this wasn't MY house that he was trespassing into. I made sure that I sat in the armchair facing the front door so that nobody could sit beside me. The tall thin man sat to my left on the couch and muscles stood in the archway leading to the front door. I suppose he was the brawn so I couldn't escape but fear kept me frozen in place.

"We are SGP My name is Agent Adams and my partner over here is Agent Hughes." Hughes gave a brief, curt nod. "We know that you've been having visions and want to discuss what that means to us. As you know we are a governmental agency that protects those with supernatural powers, such as yourself. We use them to win wars so lives are spared. We use them to negotiate treaties and for keeping peace. Your visions could assist us in our goal of world peace. What do you think so far?"

As wonderful as this sounded, I didn't believe a word coming out of his mouth. Luca had no reason to come find me or to lie to me. If the horrible things he had told me about this group were true, I didn't find manipulation and deceit to be unethical for them. I shifted in my seat trying to mull over the proper response but before I could speak, Agent Adams was talking again.

"You are worried and hesitant to answer. My ability is to read emotions. You are distrusting and don't believe that I am telling you the truth. Does that sound about right?" I managed a subtle nod. "I thought so." He continued as Agent Hughes cleared his throat. "Ahh. It appears your father is about to pull in. We don't want to startle him. Not yet anyway because I think after a few days, you're going to call, Gemma. And you're going to be interested in what we have to offer. Take my card."

Agent Adams handed me his business card before standing and walking toward the front door. "Oh and, Gemma? This won't be the last you hear of us. We are watching and we will be in touch. We can promise you that. Tell Luca, Adams and Hughes say hello. Trust me. He will remember us." A devilish smile spread across his face and a menacing chuckle escaped his lips.

The door clicked shut behind them as I sprinted to the window trying to see what vehicle they had come in but they just... vanished. How is that even possible? Shaking my head, I realized that this is a question I have been asking myself far too frequently lately. I grabbed for my cell phone and typed out a quick text to Luca. I was too scared to call out of concern that they'd be listening in. "JUST RECEIVED A VISIT FROM ADAMS AND HUGHES. THEY KNOW YOU ARE HERE AND THAT WE ARE IN CONTACT."

After hitting send, I heard my dad's car door shut. I ran to the door throwing my arms around him as soon as he walked over the threshold.

"Gem. You all right?" He patted my back a few times and pulled me back to look at my face. I didn't even realize I was crying until seeing the tear stains on his shirt. "Honey, is everything okay? Was it that boy you hung out with today?" I had to laugh at this. Of course the one and only time I have ever hung out with a boy alone, my dad automatically assumes he is the reason behind my tears. Typical overprotective father.

"No, Dad! Not at all. He was actually… great. I am just happy to see you. It has been a long day." I couldn't believe I started this morning saying goodbye to my best friend and now I was here receiving threats in my own living room. Things are changing so fast around here my head might spin.

"So then… tell me about this boy. Should I be worried?" He scratched his chin thoughtfully and looked at me like he was suspicious.

"He is just helping me with some stuff, that's all. Nothing like that!"

"Well… as long as that stuff isn't like… studying for anatomy and physiology or anything like that? I'll hire you a tutor if necessary." I felt my face turn beet red as he doubled over laughing. For just a few moments I had forgotten all about my visitors that had just left, about Grace, and about all the other things clouding my mind. That was, until I felt my phone vibrate and I remembered the text I had sent just before he walked in the door.

"All right, kiddo. I think I am going to order a pizza for dinner. I am not up to the task of cooking a thing. Not even scrambled eggs. Sound good?" He starts to loosen his tie as he hangs his keys on the hook.

"Yeah, that's cool. I'll be in my room until then." Clutching my phone to my chest, I scurried up the stairs to my bedroom and shut the door. I look around at my pale purple walls, the white full-size bedframe over in the corner beneath the window, the comforter with the little purple tulips embroidered, and once again, I wish that my mom was sitting there with open arms waiting for me. Once again, snapping me out of my reverie, my phone vibrated.

"WE NEED TO TALK THEN. AND SOON. WHEN ARE YOU AVAILABLE AGAIN? ARE YOU OKAY? – L." Sigh. I suddenly felt like I had a twenty-four-seven bodyguard but about twenty minutes ago, I realized that I needed one.

"I AM NOT AVAILABLE UNTIL TOMORROW. MY DAD IS HOME AND IF HE WAKES UP AND I AM GONE AGAIN THEN HE WON'T BE AS FORGIVING THIS TIME. I AM FINE. JUST A LITTLE STARTLED."

Not even waiting for a reply, I silenced my phone and put it on the charger next to my bed. What I really needed, was some fresh air and, luckily, I remember hearing on the radio this morning that there were some showers rolling in. Showers always meant that there would be a cool breeze in their wake. I unlatched the window and opened it enough to watch the curtains start to blow. I laid back on my bed and stared at the ceiling until I heard the doorbell and listened as my dad exchanged pleasantries with the delivery driver. Mustering up all the energy I had, I trudged to the door to make my way down for dinner, leaving my window open in hopes that a fresh breeze would cleanse away my worries.

After dinner, Dad and I decided to sit on the couch and watch a little TV. He decided on a baseball game while I lounged on the other end acting interested. I usually loved watching sports with my dad. I could name players, positions, teams, and knew the rules but tonight my head wasn't in it. I decided I would just retire to my room and open the book I have been trying to finish for the last couple of weeks. I gave him a hug goodnight and headed up. By now the rain was softly hitting the roof and there was some thunder off in the distance.

I walked into my room and instantly noticed that the window had been closed. Before I could react, a hand clamped over my mouth stifling a scream.

"Shhh shhh, Gemma. It's me. It's Luca. Don't freak out!" I ripped his hand away and spun to face him. I had to keep it down before my dad heard so I whisper-yelled the best that I could.

"Don't freak out! You snuck in my room and just grabbed me from behind! Don't freak out! That is like... like telling the runner not to run the bases after hitting a homerun!" Luca's face changed and I could tell he was trying not to laugh at me. "This isn't funny, Luca!"

"No it isn't but did you just really make a baseball reference? I just didn't peg you for being into sports." He crossed his arms and peered down at me mockingly. He could be so arrogant. We met just four days ago and yet he thinks he knows me.

"I know sports. I run. And there may or may not have been a game on downstairs before I came up but that is beside the point." He was making me flustered and I could barely string a complete thought together. "Why are you in my room anyways?" He crossed over and sat on my bed facing me.

"I told you I needed to talk to you and soon. Also, you have two men stalking you and show up at your door today. Then you just decide to leave the bedroom window unlocked and open? Are you asking to be abducted?" I hated that he was right.

"I should've been more careful. I didn't think about it. I'm sorry but that wasn't an invite for you to just whisk your way in here." I gestured from the window where he entered to the bed where he now sat. A smile played across his lips. I had seen him smirk but I hadn't seen a real smile yet.

"Sorry, princess. I will at least knock next time. But in my defense, you weren't answering my text messages and I was worried. I was able to pick up on your conversation with your dad so I knew you were alive but I just needed to see for myself. Up close." Were those butterflies in my stomach? I had never had them before. Except for in fourth grade when Connor Mitchell told me I was pretty. It was similar to the feeling of when you ride a rollercoaster and you're hanging over the edge looking at the ground, and next thing you know, your stomach is in your throat. Then I realized that my life was currently hanging over the edge threatening to spill over and I needed to focus.

"Don't call me princess. I don't need saving." Frustrated, I put my hands on my hips. I don't like the feeling of helplessness or being treated like I am fragile.

"Oh I know. I saw the light saber in your closet." Now my face was really flushed. He went in my closet?

"Well privacy must not be a word in your vocabulary. Don't sift through my things! Now let's get this over with so I can go to bed! What do you want to know?"

"Everything. Tell me everything."

He leaned back on his elbows as I paced back and forth detailing my encounter with Adams and Hughes. It was hard to concentrate. I had never had a boy in my room before. But, after I finished, I finally stole a look at him. Saying he was tense is an understatement.

"You know all that is a lie right? You can't trust them. They will tell you whatever it is you want to hear to get you on their side! They are fearing that the alliance is growing stronger!" He was on his feet now raking his hands through his hair, tugging on the ends.

"I know all that. I don't trust them. I trust you but now I am worried that they know you're protecting me or that you've been hanging around me. What if they come after you?" He looked at me and visibly relaxed just a little bit.

"I am not at all concerned with that. They won't come near me again. Not after last time. Keep your window locked and your phone on in case I need to get in touch with you. Got it?" He swung one leg out the window and waited for my response.

"Yeah I got it. Now get out of here before my dad hears you, or worse, comes in and sees you escaping through my window like a convict."

"Oh, princess… I know the situation is very serious. But you need to loosen up just a bit here and there. See you tomorrow." Then he slid out and was standing on the roof pointing at the window. I rolled my eyes and stomped over to latch it. He certainly was pushy. I watched him descend down the tree by my window

I was in a room that resembled a surgical room of sorts. There was a chair in the center with cuffs for wrists and for the ankles, a piece at the head for strapping it down too, and a large light above it. There were stainless steel cabinets all shut tight like they were holding dark secrets in them. The walls were painted the same sea foam green as the last dream I had with the same tile floors.

I heard a commotion out in the hallway and it was getting closer and closer. It sounded like a scuffle with some yelling. When the door opened there was a small, cloaked figure, Hughes and Adams, and they had someone with a bag over their head that they were dragging in. The figure was fighting back as best he could. They put him in the chair with their backs to me so I couldn't see what was going on. Once he was strapped in, they stepped back. The cloaked figure walked over to the head of the table and yanked off the bag.

I felt my heart ache as I saw Luca sitting before me. He was angry, his face was red, and the veins in his neck were protruding. The cloaked figure spoke first.

"Tell us, Luca. Where is the girl that you've been guarding? Where did you put her?" It was a female voice. One that I felt like I knew but that I couldn't place.

"I refuse to tell you. You aren't going to touch a hair on her head. Do you understand me?" The cloaked figure let out a little chuckle and I felt the hairs on my body rise.

"My dear boy, do you think that her allegiance would really lie with you if she knew the truth? Do not be ignorant. You are putting your life on the line for someone who wouldn't even choose you. So why don't you wise up and tell me where Gemma is."

"You don't even deserve to speak her name after all you've done," Luca spat, "and you better believe that I will tell her the truth because she deserves to know. But I will not give her up no matter what you do to me." The cloaked figure took a few steps back and signaled with her hand to Hughes who walked forward.

Luca reached for his head in agony but couldn't break free of what bound him. He screamed and writhed in pain. Whatever was happening to him, wasn't visible on the outside so I couldn't know what he was feeling. After a few moments, he went still.

The cloaked figure spoke again. "Bring in Elijah. I'm done here. And find me that girl." The three of them walked out the door and once it was closed, I crossed the room in seconds to reach Luca. I brushed his hair back from his face but he didn't open his eyes.

"Luca. Luca please. Luca please look at me! Please. You have to open your eyes, Luca!"

There were hands on me now, real ones, and I was jolted awake by his voice.

"Gemma. It's okay. I am here. Don't worry. You are safe." I sat up and he wrapped his arms around me with one hand on the back of my head. I was sobbing uncontrollably into his shoulder, too relieved that he was physically here to care about how embarrassing it was. I was also happy to know that it wasn't a dream where I dropped in. But does that mean it was a vision instead?

"You were dragged into a room. Strapped into a chair. They were torturing you but you wouldn't tell them where to find me. Hughes was there and he did something to you. Adams was there too and some woman that I couldn't see. She was in a robe of some sort. Your eyes closed and I couldn't get you to open them again! Then you woke me up so now I don't know… I don't know if you are okay." The words came out in a rush and I was trying to catch my breath.

"But I am okay. I am right here with you in your bedroom where you're safe." Then Luca went still and I could see from the moonlight shining on his face that something had just occurred to him. "You mean… you think it was a vision? One that you didn't get to finish so you don't know what my outcome was? If I lived or died?"

I solemnly nodded as he released me and stood up.

"Listen. Don't worry about me, okay? I know how to handle myself with those guys. Just get some rest. I can stay here a few more minutes if you'd like?" I nodded before scooting down further into my bed and pulling the blankets up tight around my neck. As haunted as I felt, there was something calming about Luca's presence. It made me not afraid to close my eyes or scared to see what would come once I did. I could rest assured that he was safe here in my bedroom.

He took a seat on the other side of the room in my rocking chair. It belonged to my mom but now I used it when I was reading. He made the chair look even smaller than it already was but it didn't seem to faze him. I closed my eyes with Luca being the last thing I saw before drifting off to sleep.

When I awoke the next morning, I checked the chair but it was empty. I had no idea what time he slipped out or how he had even managed to slip in. I know I had locked my window latch before going to bed. I checked my phone and saw I had a missed text from him an hour ago at 7.22 a.m.

"HOPE YOU GOT SOME SLEEP. DIDN'T WANT TO WAKE YOU WHEN I LEFT. TEXT ME WHEN YOU ARE UP AND I WILL COME GET YOU. IF YOU ARE UP FOR IT? – L."

"I AM UP. WHEN SHOULD I BE READY?" There were those dreaded butterflies again. Luca was my protector. Nothing more. A guy like him had to have his pick of girls and I had never dated in my life. Surely someone that looked like he belonged on the cover of *Vogue* would never have an interest in someone like me. I could barely apply my eyeliner in a straight line. What am I thinking? I am totally getting ahead of myself here. My phone vibrates again.

"SEE YOU AT 9.30. – L."

Chapter 4

"Seriously though, where are you taking me?" We were cruising in a red Honda Civic. Apparently, the Audi was his mom's and after the SGP realized we had been hanging out, we had to switch up our mode of transportation. There was a black leather jacket in the backseat, a pair of Jordans, and a book on philosophy. There seemed to be so many layers to Luca and I had only seen the surface. Apparently, under the tough, arrogant, compassionate layer there was philosophical and athletic too. Or so I assumed.

"I think it is time for my mom to meet you. She has been begging me to meet the girl that has her own bodyguard service. She also made a pact with your mom once that she would watch out for you and vice versa if anything were to ever happen to them." He didn't add anything else and then turned up the music. We went from modern rock yesterday to some Nirvana today. I gazed out the window as he drove us to the outskirts of town. We were taking winding roads that I didn't know existed.

Meeting his mom seemed like a big deal when I had only known him for five days but someone that used to befriend my mom was definitely someone that I wanted to meet. I couldn't help but get my hopes up wondering if maybe she had some answers that I had been longing for. I had just found out yesterday that my mom had hidden a whole life from me with her abilities. Now that I had developed some, it would have been great to have her to confide them to. It was a bittersweet feeling that my mom and Luca's mom had been close enough to ask that the other protect their kids. It only helped me to realize just how serious this situation really was and made me pray that my mom was okay.

As we ascended a steep hill I noticed that there wasn't much around us. The trees were thick and the wind was cooler here from all the shade fooling me into thinking it was more like October and less like July. We suddenly had left paved road and I could hear the crunch of gravel beneath the tires. I watched as Luca extended his hand to turn down the music.

"My mom doesn't like me listening to it so loud. She thinks I will blow my eardrums out or some crap like that and feels that with my ability to hear that I should be more careful. That and she worries that I will become distracted and wrap my car around a tree." With this he rolled his eyes like a typical kid living under their parents' roof and I cleared my throat as my thoughts raced to Grace just a few short days ago. "Oh my God, I am such an idiot. I am sorry, Gemma. I wasn't even thinking about your friend. I… my mom lost a sister the same way so she really worries about me driving. That was a really stupid and insensitive thing for me to say." He reached over and patted my hand that was on my lap absentmindedly and then put his hand back on the wheel. He left my skin burning in his wake.

"It's okay. I know you didn't mean any harm by it… woah." Woah was all I could say. We were pulling up to Luca's house and it was breathtaking. It came to a strong, tall peak in the middle with windows that filled the front side. From the car I could see a big fireplace dead center in the house. Everything was wood and white. White décor with the wood walls, a giant wooden light hanging from the high vaulted ceilings, and it matched perfectly with the white exterior with cranberry red shutters and door. I felt like I had just walked into a magazine. As we climbed out, it sounded like a little creek was running wild somewhere. I had never seen a place more peaceful, except for maybe the lake from yesterday. Luca and his mom definitely desired privacy and to keep to themselves.

We climbed the steps to the front door and I could see his mom jogging from the back of the house toward us, dish towel in hand. She threw open the door and I was startled because she was even more beautiful than the dream that I had. Her blonde hair matching Luca's with the bright blue eyes, perky nose, high cheekbones, and flawless skin. She smiled and I thought for sure she has done a teeth whitening commercial in her lifetime. I had never felt more ordinary in my whole life.

"Gemma! I am so excited that I am finally getting to meet you. I have been anticipating this for the last six years, since I met your mom. Oh gosh, I am getting ahead of myself. I am Darcy, Luca's mom. Please come in. I hope you two are hungry! I was just whipping up brunch. Make yourself right at home." I can see where Luca gets his strikingly good looks.

"Thank you so much for having me. Is there anything I can help you with in the kitchen?" Darcy flaps her hands as if to say oh forget it before telling me I am a guest and to just relax. After she disappeared back to the right of the fireplace, all I could do was look around. The house didn't even look like it could have been lived in. Everything here was absolutely immaculate.

"Don't tell me you're nervous, princess." Luca bumped me with his shoulder before taking a seat on the couch.

"Stop calling me that. And of course I am nervous! I am meeting your mother and your home looks like it came from an HGTV special." I looked around at all the art on the walls but realized there wasn't a single family picture in the house. Odd.

"You shouldn't be nervous. It isn't like you're my girlfriend or anything." Well that stung more than I had anticipated. "She is just excited to finally put a face to your name after all she has heard about you." I glanced at him and put my hands on my hips.

"Oh? You talking about me?" I tried to feign like I was teasing him but I really was dying to know the answer. He snorted at this which was not at all reassuring.

"Negative. She heard a lot about you from your mom. Remember?" Now I felt like an idiot and knew my face had gone fifty shades of red. Was it just me or was the room suddenly fifteen degrees hotter? Thankfully Darcy snapped me out of my embarrassment when she joined us in the living room.

"Ready, kids? I hope you like sausage and eggs. I made a breakfast casserole with biscuits and fresh fruit!" I followed behind her into the dining room that was directly behind the giant fireplace with windows that looked out onto a patio that was surrounded by woods. I looked at the spread on the kitchen table. There was a glass casserole dish in the center that smelled amazing, a big glass bowl of mixed fruits, a basket of biscuits, and a glass vase of orange juice, water, and a coffee pot. I couldn't believe she did all this just because I was coming over? Was it all for me?

Luca must've sensed that I had no idea where to sit. He moved to my left and pulled the chair out for me. I noticed Darcy look at him and give him a smile that I couldn't read. Maybe she was just grateful he was being polite to me since she knew my mom? I took my seat and Luca sat to my right with his mom at the head of the table to my left.

"So, Gemma. I have to say I am sorry about your mom. Genevieve was so amazing and loved you so much. I can't believe how much you favor her! Same auburn hair and green eyes." She smiled and took a bite. "There must be things that you are dying to know. I am sure that my son isn't the most thorough on explaining things. He tends to be a man of few words if he can help it." She winked at Luca and I shifted in my seat, unsure of where the conversation should go.

"Actually, yes I do have a couple questions. Luca said that my mom had the ability to see things that weren't there. Was that true? Did my dad know because I haven't talked to him about what is going on with me?" I looked down at my plate, ashamed that I hadn't even told the only family I had left what I was dealing with.

"Yes. Your mom is so incredibly gifted! She can paint an image and make you feel like you're really there. I remember when I was discussing with her about moving and she painted this beautiful town, the scenic view, and the life that Luca and I could live. I felt as if we were already living it and she was so spot on. The happiness I felt in that moment doesn't even compare to the happiness I feel here now. And, as for your dad, I think he did know. She told me it was best to be open about our gifts with the people that we hold nearest and dearest to us. I shared mine with Luca and his dad. His dad wasn't as open-minded about it as I once thought he would be. But as far as I know, your dad always knew your mom was special." I chewed my food slowly pondering my next question carefully.

"Do you know where my mom went?" Darcy's facial expression softened, as if it could soften any more and I knew that I had my answer then.

"I'm sorry, sweetie. I wish I had the answer for you but everyone at the Alliance is wondering the same thing. Nobody has heard from her since she took off that day and, for whatever reason, nobody can track her using her talent any more either."

I smiled more for her sake than mine. "I just thought it wouldn't hurt to ask." The rest of brunch passed with small talk. I learned that Darcy used to be an engineer with NASA, they had a beautiful house on the river in Cocoa Beach where Luca learned to surf after he learned to swim, and she loved cooking. She learned about my AP classes, the books I enjoy reading, that I run track, and she asked how my dad was doing. The conversation was light and flowing. Nothing too serious came up again and after we had finished, I tried to help her clear the table.

"Please, sweet girl, do not worry about touching a thing. You are a guest. Luca, why don't you show her around while I tidy things up?" We walked out the backdoor, down the patio, and started down a beaten path in the woods. The sound of the creek was getting louder and I knew we were approaching it.

"I hope none of that was too awkward. My mom is so warm and loving that she sometimes comes on a little too strong." He put his hands in his pockets and walked in step beside me.

"It wasn't awkward at all. She is really sweet. Also, I forgot to say thank you for staying with me last night. You really didn't have to do that." Luca shrugged. "How'd you manage to get in? I could've swore you watched me latch the window." We had reached the edge of the creek and Luca took a seat on a bench next to the water's edge. I hesitated a second before taking a seat next to him.

"It really wasn't a big deal and to be honest, I don't know how I got in. I was down the street shooting around on the basketball courts. I knew nobody was lurking around but I didn't want to leave you unattended after your little visit yesterday. And then I heard you crying out for me. I don't know how I managed to make it to your house so fast but when I made it up to your window, I just pushed and it gave. I could clearly see that it was locked but for whatever reason, it just opened. I really can't explain it." I could tell he was being honest and it troubled him that he didn't have a more definite answer. For a few minutes, we just sat in silence. The sound of the water running over the rocks was calming and it was the most at peace I had felt in a long time. Silences with Luca weren't uncomfortable like you'd expect from someone you barely know. It was like there was a natural connection that we didn't feel the need to talk, which was nice because Grace always did a majority of the talking and I wasn't a huge talker myself.

"Well regardless of how it happened, I was really glad you were there. I was afraid it was one of those drop in dreams where it was really happening. They kept talking about a truth and how if I knew what the truth was, I wouldn't pick you. I would pick them. Do you know what that means?" I glanced over at him to try and read his reaction. His face was twisted in confusion like he was searching his mind to find where any misinformation may be hidden.

"I honestly can't think of anything. I have been honest and you just have to ask, I will tell you. I don't want to keep secrets about something as big as what you're up against."

'I just have one question. My visions and these dreams... they aren't even in my control. What makes me so valuable to them that they are so interested?" I couldn't help but wonder what would make me so appealing when there were people out there like Luca, Darcy, and my mom. Surely someone has to have visions other than me.

"Your mom. She was heavily pursued by them and I think they know the connection between you two. I don't think you've reached your full potential yet and I think they are aware of that as well. There is more to you than you know." I turned to face

Luca and found he was staring back at me. It was an intense, hold your breath, don't break eye contact because you don't want to miss this moment kind of stare.

"I've only ever been ordinary. I just blend into a crowd. I have about as many layers as a banana. There isn't anything hiding deep beneath the surface." I tried to lighten the mood because, despite how serious this conversation was, I sensed something greater happening here.

"Gemma. Please stop saying you're ordinary. That is the furthest thing from the truth." Suddenly Luca was leaning in. He placed his hand on my cheek and caressed my face with his thumb. Our eyes were locked and then I felt his lips on mine. It was a soft and lingering kiss but I felt electricity flowing through me just ready to explode. It extended down my fingertips, to my toes, and I felt like I could feel every atom in my body. I was more aware of the sounds surrounding us. There were birds chirping in the distance, the sound of insect wings buzzing, the smell of the damp Earth under our feet. It was like my body was suddenly engulfed in flames. But then it was over and Luca was pulling away.

"I'm… I don't…" he kept starting but was unable to finish his sentence. He was embarrassed and regretting the decision to kiss me. He probably just did it out of sympathy and guilt because I am so pathetic sitting here and blubbering on about being only ordinary. I put my head in my hands.

"Please. Just don't finish that thought. If it is an apology you are about to utter, just forget it even happened." I stood to start walking back to the house. The high I had just felt quickly dissipated realizing that my first kiss was with someone who didn't want to kiss me at all. Before I could take a step, Luca's hand grabbed my wrist.

"I wasn't going to apologize. It's just that... I haven't felt that before. Did it feel like you were... I can't put it into words. I have kissed girls, quite a few in Florida, but nothing has ever felt like that." Luca clears his throat

"Oh... umm. Yeah I felt a lot of things but I've never been kissed before so I didn't know that it wasn't normal." Luca looked up at me in shock and then for a brief second, I think he actually blushed and a sheepish smile broke out on his handsome face.

"If it makes you feel better, I certainly couldn't tell. What did it feel like to you?" Well this was absolutely humiliating but something about the look of curiosity in his eyes told me that he genuinely wanted to know and it wasn't to inflate his ego.

"I felt everything. Like every molecule flowing in my body and my senses felt heightened. I could hear wings, smell nature, and it was like my blood was lava flowing through my veins." He smiled a big smile.

"You nailed it. I felt it too. It was unnatural but not at the same time. Like our chemistry is perfectly in line. I really can't describe it but I felt... like I had been jolted awake." We stared at each other a few more minutes in wonder before he got to his feet. "Let me show you the rest of the house." I fell into step beside him and as we walked back to the house, he was the chattiest he's ever been. I learned about his friends back home, his dog Bruno that he had left with his dad, about the philosophy he loved to read. He showed me his bedroom that was painted a nice shade of blue with a navy-blue comforter, hardwood floors to match the rest of the house, a basketball jersey hung on the wall, and an impressive bookshelf filled with books about space, sports, poetry, and just a little bit of everything else.

Despite what else is going on in my life right now, holding

his hand on the drive home and him kissing each finger before I exited the car made me feel like the sun was shining brighter and it was washing away the storms I had weathered the last few days. I climbed out of the car and made my way to the door, noticing that my dad's car was home so I couldn't snag another kiss before Luca left, and turned to watch the red Honda pull away. For the first time in days, I felt safe and optimistic. Sure, I had only shared a kiss and a little hand holding with Luca but there was something brewing that I couldn't put my finger on.

I climbed into bed not realizing how tired I was. The charade of sitting with my dad and not bringing up my mom was wearing on me. I had told him everything my whole life, even the things that dads didn't want to know. But this? I couldn't manage to look him in the eyes and ask him what he knew about her and her "gifts". Every time I played it through my mind, it came out accusatory or like I was angry with him. Deep down though, I think I was a little bit angry that he had kept it from me all these years. But I also felt guilt. Guilt for punishing him when my mom was the one that had left and she was the one that had decided to keep it from me the fifteen years leading up to her departure. I am sure my dad did it to protect me and shield me away from the other things out there, not realizing that I too could inherit some sort of supernatural... thing.

    I couldn't figure out if this thing was truly a gift or if it was a curse. Given that two out of my three dreams/visions weren't good ones, I was currently leaning more toward a curse. However, without this "curse", I wouldn't have found Luca. There was something different about our attraction. Though I had no experience in the dating field, this much I knew to be true. I had pictured my first kiss plenty of times as all the other girls in school were going on dates, getting boyfriends, and lip locking through an entire movie that their parents thought they actually went to watch, but never did I ever think that it would feel like that.

Up until today, I figured he looked at me as a project, someone to protect, a nuisance like that gnat flying around your face that you can't seem to shake but then he touched my face and I don't know where that leaves us. As if right on cue, my phone vibrated on the nightstand lighting up the whole room.

"GOODNIGHT AND SWEET DREAMS. DON'T LET THE VISIONS BITE. – L."

Chapter 5

I awoke to a new day, a Wednesday to be exact, and I hadn't had a single bad dream or vision all night. I dreamt of my mom. It had been a while since I saw her in my sleep but it was a welcome sight. She was standing in the kitchen making her famous French toast and wearing her pink and white plaid apron that still hung in the pantry. It was my grandma's and held a lot of sentimental value to both of us. She was smiling when I walked in and it was as if nothing had ever happened, like she had never left us at all. She talked about needing to get things for my upcoming graduation and wanting to arrange for senior pictures. It was like what a normal morning would consist of if she were still here, but she wasn't. That was the worst part about dreaming of her. I knew I eventually had to wake up and when I opened my eyes, she wouldn't be there.

I rolled over and heard my dad shut the front door, his key sliding into the lock, and the sound of the deadbolt rolling over. He was gone for the day. I remembered him mentioning yesterday having a few houses to show and needing to spend some time at the office today for marketing so I knew the day was all mine. I swung to my feet and started making my way downstairs when there was a soft knock on the door. I peered through the peephole and out the window but didn't see a single person or a car. I slowly pulled the door open to take a look around. There on the door mat stood a venti Starbucks cup, "Princess" was written on the side in thick black sharpie, and a slice of banana bread. I couldn't help the smile that radiated off my face and I hoped wherever Luca was sitting right now, he could see it.

I took the stairs two at a time heading for my room when I noticed the window open again. I spun around and out walked Luca from the closet.

"You've really got to quit sneaking up on me!"

"It was just too easy. I wanted to surprise you and catch you off guard. See what you look like when you've just rolled out of bed." He flashed me a smile that could melt glaciers and I felt my face warming from the blush creeping up my chest into my neck and flooding my cheeks.

"Well... here it is." I waved my hand in front of me with my black running shorts and yellow tank top that was still askew. I was silently thankful I dressed before heading downstairs this morning.

Luca looked me over. "Yep. You're still a princess."

"Why do you keep calling me that?"

"Now why does it have to be offensive? Princess Leia was both princess and Jedi badass." Luca looks at me taken aback, feigning offended, with his hands held up in front of him. I can't help but smile.

"Point taken. It can stay."

Luca smirked. I don't know what transpired over the last twenty-four hours but I liked his joking nature and carefree attitude despite what we are up against right now. Although, since my visit a few days ago, it's been relatively quiet.

"How about you get dressed and let me take you somewhere. I have someone new I want you to meet."

"Another field trip?" I groaned in protest. All I was hoping to do today was crawl in my chair with a book. The one thing that has always managed to take me away from my stresses has been neglected for far too long. I threw myself on the bed and pulled a pillow over my face.

"I know you won't be disappointed. Please? For me?" How was it that I had known Luca for a total of five days. In those five days he had become my only friend (if you could even call him that), my first kiss, and someone that I truly wouldn't mind spending every spare second with. He was mysterious but, as time went by, I got to catch a glimpse here and there of what he really was like. I threw the pillow off my face to find him leaning over me.

"Fine. I will meet you downstairs in five. But only because you have buttered me up with coffee and breakfast."

He bent down, planting a kiss on my forehead.

"Take all the time you need. I'll be downstairs snooping through any old family albums I can find." He chuckled and left the room. I jumped up kicking myself into hyperdrive before he could find any potential blackmail. I threw my hair up, tossed on a white shirt, black shorts, and my black and white Converse before heading down to find Luca sitting in my living room. Something about seeing him there made me feel like he belonged there. He was relaxed with his arm slung over the back of the couch, legs crossed, and phone in hand.

"Ready?" he asks, tucking his phone away. I nod my head in response, slinging my bag over my shoulder. I didn't care much for purses so my go to was a backpack with my wallet, a book, sunglasses, and chap stick. He strolls over to the front door where I am awaiting him, placing his hand on mine before I could turn the door handle, and uses his other hand to tilt my chin up. I feel my breath catch as he looks into my eyes. I notice the light flecks of green in his that I hadn't picked up on before.

"I barely know you, Gemma Jacobs but there is something about you. I'm not sure what it is yet but I definitely want to try and find out." Then I close my eyes as I feel his lips graze mine softly, back and forth, before he plants a kiss. Once again, he lingered, but didn't press for any more than that. And, like before, things became a little clearer. As much as the butterflies swarmed me, I could still hear the trash truck down the road, I could hear the sound of the neighbor locking their door as they head off to work, I could smell his woodsy cologne, and the scent of coffee from my dad this morning was still hovering in the house.

This time when the kiss ends, he just smiles at me and says, "Whatever that is, whatever is happening, I could get used to it." I put the key in the lock and shut the door behind us.

Luca drove us back out to the spot at the lake that he had taken me to just two days ago. I still couldn't wrap my head around the calm serenity of it and with some slight cloud coverage, it looked even prettier than it did in the sunlight. The shadows around the lake from the large trees gave it an eerie feel and you could smell the rain that would be rolling in before long. Thankfully I wore the right shoes and didn't trip on the short hike. Stumbled? Yes. But tripped? I held my own.

Once we reached the water's edge, I noticed that someone was approaching from down the shoreline. My instincts kicked in and I grabbed Luca's arm, dragging his attention to me and away from the scenery.

"There is someone heading toward us. This area is secluded. How do they know where to find us?" He looked up and chuckled.

"That is just Demora. That is who I brought you here to meet." I turned back around and took the opportunity to evaluate her. Her long gray hair was braided to the side, she was tall and willowy. She had wide eyes that looked to be the same shade as her hair. Her long sundress billowed in the wind around her. She was graceful and free.

"Luca. I am so thrilled to see you again. How is your mum doing?" I pick up on an English accent as she leans in to kiss him on both cheeks.

"She is doing fine, thank you for asking. Demora, this is Gemma." She turned her eyes on me and smiled. I instantly felt calm around her, relaxed, like I had known her forever. She then kissed my cheeks too.

"Gemma. Luca tells me you are just learning about your abilities and that you may be able to use some help in navigating them. That is where I come in. Has he told you what mine is?" I looked from Luca to Demora and shook my head no.

"I am able to help you channel your abilities, hone in on them, and learn to control them. Do you feel at ease in my presence?" I shook my head yes this time. She continued. "Good. That is another one of my specialties. I am able to calm any tensions in a room so that logical thinking can take place. Doesn't sound like it would always come in handy but, trust me, it does. I helped Luca here when they moved up this way and joined the Alliance."

"You're a part of the Alliance too?"

"Oh goodness, yes, my dear. I am one of the original founders. I worked very closely with your mum and was curious when I would get to cross paths with you. So terribly sorry she isn't around to assist you but I know she would have loved for me to help you fulfill your potential." I was never going to get used to meeting strangers that knew my mom. It was especially a tough pill to swallow knowing that they knew her better than even I did. She felt comfortable enough to share her secret with these people but not her own daughter? I pushed the thoughts from my mind and again felt peaceful. Demora must've been able to sense my discomfort.

"I really appreciate you taking the time to meet us but I have only had two dreams and a vision. There isn't much to really get to the root of."

"Don't sell yourself so short. Do me a favor, would you? Close your eyes. I want you to picture yourself standing alone in one of your favorite places. Can you do that for me?"

I took a deep breath and squeezed my eyes shut. I pictured myself standing in my Grandma Gertie's living room. The smell of her famous snickerdoodle cookies was wafting in the air. The TV was on in the background and I could hear one of her soap operas playing in her sewing room. I could feel the old red carpet beneath my feet and there was the silent ticking of her grandfather clock. The wind was rustling the yellow drapes and a nice breeze flowed through the opened windows. I was getting lost in the moment when Demora's voice interrupted my thoughts.

"Very good, Gemma. I can sense you are at total peace. Now I want you to go a little deeper. I want you to envision those that you've lost standing with you in your happy place. I need you to communicate with them. Tell them whatever it is that you've been holding in." All of a sudden, Grace was in the room with me. She was sitting in my grandma's rocking chair looking as radiant as ever. To my left was Grandma Gertie, standing in the doorway to the kitchen. She was wringing her hands in her apron and smiled at me longingly. I looked to my right and there sat my mom on the bench beneath the open window. A book was open in her lap but she put her bookmark in and looked up at me expectantly. It felt so real that I could swear I could almost physically reach out and touch them. I decided to start with Grandma because she was the simplest of all. I take a deep breath and feel mildly ridiculous but here goes nothing.

"Grandma. I miss you so much. I never got to say goodbye and at the funeral, I was too afraid to approach you and touch your hand one last time. Please forgive me for not having the strength to say goodbye." Grandma moved over to me and placed her hand on my shoulder. I know I felt it there, gentle and warm. She kissed my cheek and told me she had always been with me and always would be. Next was my mom.

"Mom. I don't know why you left but I am so angry with you. You left me and Dad and never looked back. I need you most right now and you aren't here to help. I am scared and I feel alone. But I also just wish I knew that you were okay and were still out there. That way I can have hope that one day we can be reunited." She let out a sigh and came over to me. She took both of my hands in hers and I could feel the cold metal of her rings on my skin. I looked at her hands and they were just as I remembered them, smooth and tanned and kind.

"Gemma. You are stronger than you know. I have faith that when it is time for you to make the decision that is weighing so heavily on your heart right now, that you'll make the right choice. I am much closer than you think." She then kissed my forehead before fading away. I slowly walked over to Grace. This is the one that I was dreading the most.

"Grace. I am so sorry that I didn't save you. I could have and I did nothing. You should be here right now. It should have been me and not you!" I felt her embrace.

Her arms wrapped around me tight and her body was warm against mine. She didn't let go when she said, "Gemma, there was no saving me. It was just my time and there is nothing you could have done. I may not have been conscious, but I felt you there, holding my hand and caring for me. Thank you for being the best friend a girl could have ever asked for."

My eyes flew open and I could feel tears streaming down my face. I didn't even know that I was crying but I could taste them on my lips and Luca was by my side in an instant rubbing my arm and staring at me like he was waiting for something, anything. Demora's eyes were wide and bewildered like she had seen a ghost but I felt that it was in fact me who saw ghosts. We sat there in silence for what felt like eternity while I tried to regulate my breathing, wiping at my eyes trying to calm myself down.

"You are absolutely extraordinary. That was unlike anything I have ever seen. The purpose of that exercise was to help your heart feel free and take any negative energy out of your body but... I think you just tapped into an ability that you didn't know you even had." What was she talking about? I didn't understand a thing that just happened. Surely it had all been in my imagination and they didn't know what I had seen, merely bystanders while I submerged myself into a realm far beyond our grasp.

"I – I don't understand. Wasn't... wasn't that all in my mind? In my imagination?" I looked to Luca for clarity hoping he could tell me what it was that left them in such awe. "What happened?" I waited for him to answer. I needed to hear whatever it was come from his lips. He had become one of the only people I trusted over the last few days. I needed him to explain to me what was going on.

"Uhh, Gemma. Everything you imagined, we also saw and felt. We saw the house you were in and could feel a breeze, someone was baking, a knitted blanket was hanging over the floral sofa. We saw your Grandma, Grace, and your mom. We heard them talking to you and saw that they were able to touch you."

"But I didn't see you guys there. It was just the four of us in the room."

"I think you somehow projected what you were seeing without inviting us in. We weren't part of the exercise when I asked you to imagine people there with you. But you made us both see and feel what you were feeling... it is similar to your mum's abilities but... you were stronger." Demora stared at me thoughtfully. Stronger than my mom? How could that be when I am so new to this?

"What was the difference? I know nothing about her 'abilities'? I am starting to think that I didn't know her at all!" Anger was rising to the surface. It is a relatively new emotion for me. I have always been so passive and laid back but the dark family secrets have me unraveling at the seams. I feel a sense of calm wash over me again.

"Your mum could make you see things that weren't there. Play out scenarios and have them unfold before you. But never could you physically touch it. I remember she proved her talent to me by surrounding me with bears, my favorite animal. But if I reached out to touch them, my hand would go through them like a hologram. You? You can physically feel the room around you and the people you placed in that room touched you. Could you feel them?" I gave her a nod yes. "That is unheard of. I haven't ever seen anything like it."

"What about the other things? The visions and the dreams?" I felt like I had fewer answers than I came with and more questions and my anxiety was not enjoying the rollercoaster ride

I appeared to be on.

"All in time, precious. I'd love for you to come by the Alliance. We are meeting tomorrow at five thirty p.m. Are you available?" All this time Luca has been standing here quiet and thoughtful. I looked to him and he gave a curt nod, subtle, and I knew it was his way of telling me that we would go together.

"I'll be there. Thank you, Demora."

"Absolutely. Luca, you know where we are. I'll see you both tomorrow." She turned and started wandering down the coastline in the direction in which she had come. I felt immobilized but I finally turned my attention to the sky. It looked like it was about to unleash its fury and we still had a walk to make. I turned to start walking, my head so muddled with questions and confusion, my heart aching from feeling so close to people that weren't there that I missed tremendously, and wishing I had all the answers. I almost missed Luca sliding his hand into mine. He gave it a little squeeze, reassuring and strong but comforting too. We walked with only the sound of our steps before the rain started breaking through the trees. Luca, dragging my hand with him, ran for a tall tree with a thick trunk, pulling me as close to the base as possible.

I felt a shiver run over me and wrapped my arms around myself trying to muster up some warmth. I don't remember it being that cool outside but my teeth were starting to chatter. Luca wrapped his arms around me and pulled me to his chest. I hadn't noticed how well I fit there but was instantly feeling farther and farther from the brink of hypothermia.

"It is just nerves. You're okay. We will just hang here for a few until the hardest rain passes," he whispered into my ear. Before I could even process what it was that I was doing, I ran my fingers up the back of his neck and wrapped them in his hair. I had never been brave enough to make a move but right now I just needed to feel something, anything, besides this cold biting betrayal that I was feeling down to my bones.

I tilted my head up and felt the pressure of Luca's mouth on mine. It wasn't like the gentle kisses we had exchanged. This one was urgent like he needed to get lost in me as much as I was hoping to get lost in him. His hands moved to cradle my face and I stepped as far into him as I could. He parted my lips and deepened the kiss. There was a hunger behind it and one of his hands slid to the small of my back, pulling me closer. He took a step and turned us, pressing me against the rough bark of the tree. I still had the one hand tangled in his hair and the other wrapped around his waist. Despite how heated this moment felt, once again I was aware of everything around us. The sound of the dew drops sliding down the leaves, the squirrels taking cover in the branches above us, and way off in the distance there was a boat that was trying to get out of the direct path of the storm.

I was lost in the moment and felt euphoric. This was unlike anything I had ever experienced before. As I was giving myself over to the pleasure in his kiss, his touch, his warm body against mine, I felt a vision that was coming on and this one wasn't in my dreams. I was standing by Luca's car wearing the same clothes I am in now. I look over to Luca and see he also hasn't changed. The car is wet from the rain that just passed and as Luca reaches to open my door, it is suddenly slammed shut. We turn and find Agents Adams and Hughes are standing there. Hughes leaned up against the car with his arms crossed, sunglasses shielding his eyes (which were totally unnecessary as it was overcast and had just rained), and he looked as uninterested as I would in a game of cricket. I could tell he was a man of very few words. Before anyone could speak, I broke the trance thrusting me back into the present.

My breath is ragged and Luca has my face in his hands again. He looks concerned and I am now self-conscious not knowing what happened as I was sucked into my vision. I found my voice before Luca could speak.

"They are here. I saw them. Adams and Hughes are going to meet us at your car but I didn't see what happened after that. It was so quick that I couldn't figure out how it is going to go down." The corners of his mouth turn down and I can't tell if he is scared or angry.

"They aren't going to hurt you, you hear me? They won't touch a hair on your head, I promise. Don't be afraid and don't let them get into your head."

"I know. I won't. I trust you." I took a deep breath, took hold of his hand, and started walking back toward the car. We walked in silence, both deep in thought about what lay ahead. When we reached the car, there wasn't a sign of a single soul around. Luca looked around and noticeably relaxed as if the threat weren't present. He moved to open the car door and that was when I knew they had appeared almost as if out of thin air. Hughes slamming the door shut again.

"Gemma. Luca. Surprised to see us?" Adams appraises us with a devilish smile spreading across his face. Luca grabs for my hand and gives it a reassuring squeeze.

"Not at all. We saw you coming. What do you two want? Couldn't find any other innocent teenagers to torture with your presence?"

"Oh come on now, Luca. You may have escaped us but that doesn't mean we can't put you through what we did last time. Do you need a reminder?" I stepped forward unwilling to let Luca take the abuse from them when it was me they were searching for.

"I haven't forgotten about our last conversation. You two seem awfully persistent. What is it that you want from me?" I was surprised to hear that I sounded confident and calm when inside I felt like every bone was rattling out of fear. This being my second encounter with these two, I still had no idea what they were capable of.

"You know what we want," Adams said. "We want to offer you our protection in exchange for your help."

"That is complete and total bullshit and you know it!" Luca's blood pressure is rising as the words rush from his mouth. I put a hand to his chest and wait until he makes eye contact before removing it. He picks up on my thoughts. Let me just handle this for now. There are no threats of immediate danger for the time being.

"I have made my decision and I am not interested in your 'protection'. Remove me off whatever list you're keeping and move on. I want nothing to do with your program." I squared my shoulders but didn't miss the smirk that broke out onto Hughes' face. He was still leaning against the car and looking amused.

"You see... our leader will not be happy with this news. And when our leader isn't happy, nobody is. So you won't be off our radar that easily. Actually, have you cared to share your little secret with your father?" Adams was blackmailing me?

"You leave my father out of this. He has been through plenty. It has nothing to do with him."

"It would be a shame if we were to, oh I don't know, drop by and have a little chat with him. Help him to... understand how important it is for you to join our cause. Isn't that right, Hughes?" Hughes gave a curt nod with the grin still on his face. "I'll give you one more chance to think it over, Gemma. But our leader isn't a very patient person and neither are we. So for your sake, your dad's, and your little boyfriend here... I hope you make the right decision. And, Luca? You're still on our radar too so I would be careful what you decide to meddle in." Adams nodded toward the woods and started off the way that we had just come, Hughes following on his heels.

Luca practically took the door off the hinges when he opened it, almost shoving me inside. He shut the door and locked the car as he made his way around to the driver side and then slid into the seat beside me. He started the car up and, like a scene out of *Grand Theft Auto*, he threw the car in reverse spinning us around to face toward town. Dirt and leaves went flying and we began accelerating at a high speed down the winding road.

"Slow down! They aren't even following us! You're going to end up wrecking!" I had one hand on the handle above my door and the other braced on the dash but, to my dismay, Luca didn't slow down.

"You have to pack a bag. We have to run away. They aren't going to stop until they have you. I know these guys, Gemma! They won't stop!"

"I can't just pack up and run! They will find us no matter where we go. You and I both know they have to have some powerful people on their side. I also think you're forgetting that I am only eighteen. I have responsibilities. Like graduating would be nice."

"Your responsibilities won't matter if they get ahold of you," he sneers in reply. "I need you to settle down. We can talk to the Alliance tomorrow and see what they think. Maybe they have some advice for me." A few minutes of silence passed but I could tell that his breathing was almost regular, or at least on its way to getting there. He slowed but still had a death grip on the steering wheel and his eyes glued to the road in front of us.

"Fine," he finally caved, "but I am not leaving your street tonight. You aren't going to be out of my sight. Deal?"

"Yeah, whatever. Deal. As if I could get out of your sight even if I tried." A few more minutes of silence passed us as we entered into town. I could sense that he was tense but so was I.

"I think you should tell your dad tonight. He needs to know." His tone had changed. It was serious yet cautious.

"I'm not telling him. He didn't even tell me about my mom. What if he doesn't accept me?"

"Your dad won't be like mine. I can tell. You are all that he has left." I rolled this over in my head. I should tell my dad. I hadn't ever kept secrets from him and this wasn't like an 'I backed into the mailbox' secret. This was a 'my life is possibly in jeopardy and oh yeah, I also see things' type of secret. It was huge but I worried if he was strong enough to handle it right now. Each day was still a task for him with my mom gone and the pressure he felt to pick up the slack and be both parents for me. He even tried to learn how to French braid hair after she left but I had to keep telling him that I was fine just having the best dad in the world. Usually that softened him up a bit.

As Luca continued to drive toward my house, I thought of how to break it to my dad. I hoped he would be understanding but also worried that he would think that because my mom and I have this in common, I would end up leaving him too. I didn't want him to have that fear each day that I was going to pick up and walk out. Luca was right. I was all he had and vice versa. I had been so wrapped up in my thoughts that I didn't notice we had pulled up out front of my house. My dad still wasn't home but it was only three p.m. I knew it would be only a matter of time before he was pulling in.

"Leave your window open, yeah?"

"Yeah, sure. As long as you promise not to leave the area. I don't want Hughes and Adams thinking my open window is an open invitation for them to come tell me a bedtime story." I tried to be funny but the corners of his mouth only tugged up a little bit, like he had to put a lot of effort into a smile right now. "What can Hughes do, anyway? Adams told me he can feel out and read emotions. Is Hughes just the muscle that backs him up?"

"Hughes is the most dangerous one. Man of few words but he can make you wish you were dead. He gets into your nervous system and into your body and causes you pain. He can make you feel like you're on fire, like your brain is about to explode, like your lungs are filling with water… he is the one they use to do a lot of their torturing. Doesn't talk, doesn't need the muscles, but can bring you to your knees and get the answers he wants without even getting his hands dirty." I shivered at the thought that Luca probably knows this from experience. I knew that was a conversation that was off limits so I didn't press my luck.

"Well thank you for today. I enjoyed meeting Demora and can't wait to meet everyone tomorrow." I opened the car door to go but Luca caught my hand pulling me back in. I turned to face him and he grabbed the back of my head, pulling me in for a kiss, his lips gentle against mine and sweet. A neighbor seven houses down was weed whacking his yard, the mail man was one street over placing mail in the mailbox, there was a cricket somewhere in my backyard that was gently purring, and all these things I could hear whenever Luca kissed me.

I walked in the house, checking to be sure the door had been locked and the house looked untouched, and sat on the couch with a glass of lemonade. I turned on a rerun of *Gilmore Girls* and waited for my dad to get home so I could tell him just how ordinary I indeed was not.

After we finished our chicken parmesan dinner, one of dad's specialties, I cleaned up the table and told him to go turn on a game so I could wrap up the dishes. I was trying to buy myself some time before having the conversation that I knew was necessary. It didn't make it any easier but I just needed to rip it off like a band aid and throw it all out there. I put the leftovers in the fridge, loaded the dishwasher, and wiped up the counters before joining him in the living room.

He was still in his work clothes but his shoes were off and feet up on the table. I noticed he was wearing the pink and lime green pineapple socks I had gotten him for Father's Day. He loved funky socks.

"So what did you do today, kiddo? Anything good?" He is distracted, flipping through the channels.

"I hung out with Luca. Actually, I have spent the last few days hanging out with him." I was fidgeting with my hands, worrying that this bomb I was about to drop would blow the roof off of our house.

"He seems like a nice boy. Would I know his parents?"

"Umm, I don't think so. Listen, Dad, I need to talk to you." He pauses his channel surfing and turns to me, sitting up a little straighter. Now I have his attention.

"Oh God, Gemma, please don't tell me you are thinking about furthering your relationship with him already. You can't possibly be serious enough to…"

"DAD!" I interrupted him because I was embarrassed just thinking that Luca was listening in somewhere close by. "It is NOTHING like that."

"Well… that is excellent news." The relief on his face was apparent. "What is on your mind then?"

"Did you know that... that Mom was really special?" His face softened at the mention of her.

"Of course I did, sweetheart. Why do you think I fell in love with her? She was such a special woman."

"No, I mean that she was a little MORE special than most people are?" It wasn't his fault but I was getting a little aggravated. This conversation was hard enough as it was. Could he just put the pieces together?

"What are you talking about, Gemma? Who have you been talking to?" Now it was his turn to be aggravated? Or was he scared?

"Luca's mom knew Mom. She told me about Mom's... abilities. What she was able to do."

"They had NO RIGHT to tell you those things! Your mother wanted to keep you from that life. I HAVE WANTED TO KEEP YOU FROM IT!" He was on his feet, hands in his hair, face redder than a cherry, and he was clearly very upset.

"Dad they only told me because... because I have abilities too!" He finally looked at me and then slowly sat back down. His mouth was wide open out of shock and he had been rendered speechless. He was just on a rampage and now, nothing.

"What? What can you do? Are you, I mean, is it the same thing as your mom?"

"Kind of? I have had a few visions, dreams that take me somewhere in the present, and I learned today that I am able to project my thoughts for others to see. I spent time with a woman named Demora that is going to help me." He was calm now. Calculated. Taking it all in.

"Demora? Your mom used to talk about her and how wonderful she was. Your mom trusted her with everything. I am glad you have someone helping you. Has anyone ELSE contacted you?"

"SGP has but Luca is keeping an eye on them for me. Nothing to worry about, Dad. I don't even have control of this stuff yet but I just wanted you to know. I don't like having secrets." Like the secrets you've been keeping from me for the last seventeen years and his reply is like he is reading my mind.

"I am sorry we didn't tell you. We didn't want to unless we had to. I don't know much about SGP. Your mom kept most of that stuff private to protect us both. Please know you can tell me anything. I'm sorry I kind of lost my cool there. I thought her secret left with her and we wouldn't have to ever have this discussion."

"I understand, Dad. Thanks for listening." His eyes soften and his features relax.

"Thank you for feeling you can tell me. I love you no matter what." I smiled and after a moment, he went back to watching his game but I could tell that his mind was elsewhere. I was glad the conversation was apparently over. It was quicker than I had anticipated but at least it was finally off my chest. I decided it was time to retire so I could get plenty of sleep before meeting the Alliance tomorrow. I gave him a hug, he kissed my forehead, and I stumbled up the steps.

I opened my door and there was Luca, stretched out on my bed reading *Twilight*.

"I really don't understand what all the hype was about? The man sparkles in the sun and she is just willing to give up everything for him? You know who is underrated? Charlie. Now he was a solid dad." He folds the page down to mark his spot, something that secretly irks me because I expect my books to be in perfect condition but he is so gorgeous that I will let it slide just this once.

"You've read all the books?"

"Well not exactly. I watched the movies but NOW I am reading the books. I just had to find something to distract myself from all these thoughts of… our relationship moving to the next level?" I went rigid and felt the familiar heat of a blush coming on. Luca found this quite comical and had to try to keep his laughter down.

"Relax, kiddo! I was just giving you a hard time. I was eavesdropping on your convo with your dad. Sounds like it went swimmingly by the way."

"I thought for sure he was going to lose it." I sat on the edge of the bed and felt Luca start drawing circles on the back of my hand. "I mean, he was a little angry but now I feel like he is almost a little scared or something? I couldn't get a good read but at least he didn't call me a freak so I suppose it could have gone worse."

"He knows and that's all that matters, princess. I was just coming by to tell you a quick goodnight before I take up my post at the park or down the block."

"Don't you ever get a chance to sleep?"

"Ehh, yeah, I take naps here and there. Due to my heightened senses, I am a light sleeper anyway so I know nothing will slide past me."

"That makes sense. Are you taking *Twilight* with you for some light reading?" He sprung from my bed and started toward the window.

"Only if you tell me… would I be more of a Jacob or an Edward?" It was my turn to hide the laughter.

"That is a tough one. I have always been pro Jacob Black. Wolfs are pretty legit."

"I'll take it then." He leaned in, planting a kiss on my lips, then one on my forehead, and one on each cheek before kissing my lips again. The last kiss lingered and I could hear the game on the TV downstairs. The Yankees were up by two in the bottom of the seventh. It also sounded like my dad was snoring. Luca broke the kiss, rubbed a thumb across my lips, and climbed out the window. I locked it behind him and climbed under the comforter, turning off the lamp and closing my eyes. I prayed the high that he left me with would last me through the night so I could get some good sleep. My lips were still burning from his kiss.

Chapter 6

I was sitting on a bed in a room that looked to belong to the same old hospital that I saw Luca and his mom in before. My maroon track duffel bag was beside me with some clothes in it. I was cold and shivering. Lightning lit up the room and I could hear the rain coming down and pinging on the windows. Darcy suddenly appeared and sat down beside me, putting her arm around my shoulders and rubbing to warm me.

"Don't worry. You're safe here and your dad is safe too. Everything will be all right." My dad? What did my dad have to do with this? Safe? What was going on?

"Thank you so much, Darcy. Where did Luca go?" I felt emptiness without him near. What is happening?

"He just ran back to our home to pack a quick bag. I think we are all going to stay here until this passes over or we figure out a solution. I don't want you to stress it though! The Alliance is used to handling these types of situations so hang tight and it'll get resolved. Let us handle it." She rested her cheek against the top of my head and I felt surrounded by a mother's love. The same love my mom surrounded me with and the same love I watched Grace's mom surround her with and try to show me too after my mother had left. I could feel my body start to warm and whatever tension I had been carrying was starting to dissolve.

"Darcy! It's Luca." I turn to find Demora in the doorway, body posture rigid, and eyes the size of saucers. That is when I jolted upright.

"Woah, princess. Easy now. What is it?" I feel the weight of Luca's body sitting on the edge of the bed before I visibly see him. My eyes adjust as the moonlight from the window is cast across his face. I feel a cold sweat from head to toe.

I can't respond because my whole body feels numb. I try to calm my breathing and prevent my heart from leaping out of my chest.

I feel ridiculous telling him about these visions or dreams... yeah that is what they are. Dreams. There is no reason that I would ever have to go into hiding or that my father's safety would be hanging in the balance. Is there?

"Yeah. It was just... just a nightmare," I manage to finally stutter out.

"You sure it wasn't a vision? It has you really shaking." Luca's sweet face is etched with concern and my heart swells.

"I'm just relieved to see you're okay."

I look down at my hands and take a few deep breaths to collect myself. Luca reaches out and cups my face in his hand. I lean my head into his palm and allow myself to look at him, really look at him. There are lines of worry creasing his forehead and the circles under his eyes tell me he hasn't been sleeping.

"Try and get some rest okay? I'll leave you to sleep but I will stay outside and watch over you."

"NO!" I realize I am shouting and drop my voice to a whisper. "Please stay with me. In here. I don't want to be alone." I plead with my eyes and hope that he can see the desperation that lies there.

"All right. I'll just take a seat by the window but please try to get some sleep." He stands to go and, as his hand slips away from my face, I grab ahold of him and pull him back to me.

"Just stay here. You look like you need some rest too. Maybe you can get some sleep if you're closer... you know, in case something happens?" I slide over and I can see that he is hesitant. I have never been so daring but I can't shake the feeling that this vision or dream, whatever it may be, is telling me something important. He climbs in next to me and pulls me into his arms. I rest my head on his chest and find comfort in the sound of his beating heart.

As I finally start to drift back to sleep, I can tell that his breathing has slowed and he must be asleep. I put my arm around his waist and let my heavy eyes close.

I can feel the sun on my face and as I go to stretch, I feel a foot against mine. My eyes fly open as I look over and see the peaceful and serene look on a sleeping Luca's face. As I reach to trace the curve of his lips, one sleepy eye opens and catches me with my fingers just inches from his mouth. A slow smile starts to spread before he jolts from my bed and into the closet. I am so startled that I can't even register what is happening before my dad lightly raps on my door before coming in.

"Good morning, kiddo. I didn't expect to find you awake. I was just checking on you before I stepped out for the day." I feel anxious and just want him to leave before he takes notice of the tall blonde boy in my closet. He would have a heart attack and I would be grounded until I graduated... college.

"Uhh yeah, good morning, Dad. Umm... what is on your agenda for the day?" Fingers crossed that it involves walking from my room to the door.

"Just a few appointments this morning, lunch with a client—"

"Wait. Lunch with a client? You don't normally do that?" Dad suddenly looks nervous and is looking around like he refuses to make eye contact with me. Something isn't right.

"Ahh yeah. Well she just moved to town and doesn't know anybody so I offered to take her to lunch after we looked at some properties."

"Oh… it is a she? Well… have a good time I guess." I feel nauseous and can't figure out what it is that is bothering me.

"Yeah. Thanks, Gem. I'll see you probably around five o'clock. Have a good day." I watch as he shuffles back out the door and, for whatever reason, the room feels very tense. I wasn't used to getting this kind of vibe from my dad. I am so lost in the thought of him going to lunch with a woman that I forget Luca is in the closet until the door slides open and he is standing there in my varsity letterman jacket, light saber in hand, and a neon pink sweatband on his hand from the aerobics costume I wore to a Halloween party a few years ago.

I can't help but crack a smile. "Are you enjoying your time in my closet? Find anything of interest to you?" Luca strides out of the closet like he is a model in Milan during fashion week.

"I always fancied these letterman jackets but, as a surfer, you didn't get to letter in any school sports." He looks at me and his smile falters. "I can tell that the conversation with your dad upset you. Want to talk about it?"

I shrug my shoulders. "I am not sure there is anything to even talk about. That is the problem."

Luca walks over to me and takes my hands in his. Sitting on the edge of the bed, he turns toward me and I can feel him studying my face.

"Princess. I think you are beautiful, and I am so lucky to have gotten to stay beside you all night but… . if you don't put some clothes on so we can go get breakfast, I may be forced to eat the ages old Easter candy that I found in your closet." I pick up a pillow and throw it at his head as he laughs and ducks. "Okay but seriously. I am going to run to my car to change my clothes and I will be waiting downstairs for you."

I toss back the comforter, and swing my legs over the edge of the bed. As I walk to my dresser I think about the fact that I can't remember the last time I slept so well. Butterflies in my chest, I pull a pair of jean shorts from the bottom drawer and start the walk to my closet when I hear footsteps coming up the stairs. I whip the door open. "You are so impatient! Just give me another mi—"

"Hi, Gemma. Were you expecting someone else?" Hughes and Adams are standing in my hallway staring back at me. There is no sign of Luca anywhere. I can hear my heart beating in my ears, my head suddenly feels light and dizzy, and my mouth has gone dry. "I assume you were looking for Luca. How cozy of you two to have a little sleepover. I am sure that your father wouldn't appreciate that. Maybe we should let him in on the little secret. What do you think, Hughes?"

Adams looks back and Hughes gives a curt nod.

"Where is Luca?" I ask afraid of what the answer might be.

"Ahh don't worry. He is fine. Doesn't even know that we dropped in. I am sure that he will return any moment now so let me make this quick. Our leader is growing very impatient with your lack of response."

"I did respond. I told you I am not interested. You and your leader seem to be awfully persistent and not understand the meaning of no thanks." Hughes steps forward now but is stopped when Adams places his hand on his chest before he can advance any further.

"You see, Gemma. Hughes doesn't take to anyone talking poorly of our leader so please excuse him. You are lucky that we were told not to harm you, or your friend for that matter... for now. The thing is, there is concern that if we harm Luca then you certainly won't want to join us. Our leader is quite confident though that in time, and sooner rather than later, you will realize you're wrong here. You belong with us."

"That is what YOU don't realize. I don't belong to anyone, any organization, or owe any of you anything. So if you don't mind, I have somewhere to be." Adams smirks and scratches his chin. It is like he and Hughes are mocking me.

"Oh we know. Breakfast was it? We will see you there but don't worry. You won't see us." He chuckles and turns to walk down the stairs. I watch them go before they vanish into thin air, not once even opening the front door.

I'm sliding on my last shoe when I hear the front door open and someone is bounding up the steps. Judging by the sound of the stairs and their lack of subtlety, I already know it is Luca. He throws the door open and I can't help but take him in, causing my already racing heart to quicken its pace. He is wearing dark wash jeans and a maroon V-neck with white slip-on vans. When we finally make eye contact I can tell he is worried.

"What's wrong? You look troubled. I leave for five minutes, and you have this dark cloud hanging over you. Spill it."

"Adams and Hughes were just here. You literally walked out the door and then they were in my hallway." Luca's face goes white but I can see his hands are clenched into fists. I suddenly worry that he may put his hand through my door but slowly he relaxes after a few deep breaths and closing his eyes. I give him all the time he needs and wait until he is ready to speak.

"I listened in the whole time I was gone. I didn't hear a thing. I mean... I couldn't even hear you walking around the house. I didn't see them. I did a perimeter sweep before going to my car. There is just... there has to be – how are they getting to you without me noticing?"

A thought crosses my mind. I think about the fact that I didn't hear them open the door, I didn't see them leave through the door, and they said that they would see me but I wouldn't see them. What does that even mean? I don't want to worry Luca any more than necessary but I have to be honest. I feel like we are up against something much bigger than we think.

"Luca, I think they are being shielded. Is that possible? I know I am new to this whole gifted or supernatural stuff but they were in here and then gone almost like they just vanished into thin air. What if they are shielded and... is teleporting a thing or like... beaming in?" Luca just stares at me and I now feel very self-conscious. Having visions is one thing but teleporting? That just sounds ludicrous. "I didn't realize how crazy that sounded until I said it out loud and now you're looking at me like I am Medusa and it's making me really nervous."

"No. Gemma. I think you are onto something. You're right. The times that they have shown up, I couldn't see them coming. Ever since they realized I was standing guard over you, I haven't been able to pick up on their voices or anything. I didn't even hear them in here talking to you. There has to be someone protecting them and allowing them to break through my defense." Luca is pacing, hands raking through his hair, pondering the observation I just shared with him.

"Luca, there is one more thing. They said they would see us at breakfast, but we wouldn't see them." I think this over. That is a little scary to think that I am not safe anywhere. That no matter where I am, they are listening and watching. That must mean they are watching when I sleep, when I eat, they hear our every conversation, they know that Luca is more than my security detail (even though I have no idea what more means at this point), and they know my every move. It is unsettling to realize my privacy is gone.

"Let's just go get breakfast but keep the conversation light until we can get somewhere safe to talk. We don't want to give anything more away."

We walk into Tiffany's, the family diner down the road from my house. Tiffany's is supposed to be a play on the Audrey Hepburn movie "Breakfast at Tiffany's". They only serve breakfast and they serve it all day. It has always been one of my favorite places. My mom and dad used to bring me here every Saturday before dad ran off to his real estate appointments. It was the one time every week that we knew we would all be together with no interferences. Sometimes Grace would come along too.

I look around at the white and black checkered floor tiles, the red table tops, and the black vinyl booths and chairs. To the left of the counter, there is a jukebox that my dad used to play "Folsom Prison Blues" by Johnny Cash as we waited for our order. Johnny Cash was one of my mom's favorites from when she was growing up and they used to sit on the same side of the booth singing it together. My dad would play air guitar and it used to embarrass me. To think that I would give anything to go back in time and experience those breakfasts and watch them sing that song one last time.

We take a seat as Rosie, the same waitress that used to wait on us since I was little, strolls over with the pink laminated menus. I can honestly say that the only thing that has changed about the whole place is the fact that the staff is aging. Everything else is exactly the same down to the silver napkin holder and the

Audrey Hepburn picture hanging above the service window.

"Gemma! It is so good to see you. How is your father?" Rosie always had a soft spot for my dad after my mom left. We tried to keep up the tradition of coming here but without my mom, my dad couldn't handle it. The few times that we tried ended in him barely touching his food and going home to do housework and keep his mind occupied the rest of the day. Only bonus was our house was spotless and the yard was always immaculate.

"He is doing great, Rosie. Staying busy with work as usual. How have you been?" I look at her red hair that is speckled with gray pulled back into a tight bun, her red lipstick and the way her eyes are starting to wrinkle in the corners, but they are still just as blue as they've always been. I remember the way that she used to be so excited to give me my pancakes because she would draw faces on them with whip cream and fruit, each time it was different. I got Mickey, a clown, and monkey just to name a few.

Rosie looks at Luca like she just noticed that he was sitting there.

"Well hello, sugar. And who might you be?" Luca blushes and smiles, which also leads me to blushing and I can't make eye contact with either one of them.

"I am Luca, ma'am. It is a pleasure to meet you."

"Well now, Luca, you listen. First off, I am not a ma'am. That is my mother and my older, dried up, sister Petunia. Second off, you better treat Gemma right. She is family around here."

"Yes ma— I mean yes, Rosie. I sure will." I look up to find him smiling at his menu and Rosie is listing off the special (two eggs any style, two sausage links, hashbrowns, and toast... I don't think the special has changed in the last fifteen years). After ordering two specials, my eggs over medium and his scrambled with cheese, Rosie saunters off to relay our order to the cook. She looks back over her shoulder, winks at me, points at Luca, and then gives me a thumbs up.

"About earlier with Adams and Hughes…" I trail off when Luca holds up his hand to tell me to stop.

"We aren't discussing them, nothing to do with the SGP, and certainly nothing about what we suspect. In the six days that I have known you, I feel like I have known you forever but I know nothing at all. Tell me about you. Let's consider this to be a first date. Normal teenager stuff today." Luca reaches across the table and takes my hands in both of his.

"A date? But we've already kissed, you spent last night sleeping in my bed, and I've met your mom. Don't you think that is a little backwards?" I can't help but laugh at the absurdity that is my life right now. A week ago, I had never even held hands with a boy unless you counted that time that Jake Reynolds grabbed my hand to help pull me out of the pool… I hardly think that it should count against me.

Ignoring everything I just said, Luca looks me in my eye and says, "Gemma. Thank you for meeting me this morning. I am so glad that we were finally able to get together. Please tell me about yourself." The butterflies took over and I felt that I could fly. How did this boy have me swooning so hard but I knew so little.

"There isn't much to know. I love to read books, I love the beach, when I run I like to listen to music. The usual girl stuff."

"What do you listen to when you run?"

"This may come as a surprise to you but I listen to Eminem and 80s rock. All on the same playlist. One minute I am running with Slim Shady and the next I am listening to Guns n' Roses." Luca nods his approval. "But enough about me. Tell me about YOU."

Luca clears his throat and takes up a phony British accent. "You see, madam, I like to play the piano and guitar. I love all animals except I have a fear of snakes. My zodiac sign is an Aquarius and I have rather a fondness for poetry and Shakespeare." I am speechless. He is so well rounded and down to Earth but I also can't tell if he is serious. Boys like him exist?

"Really?"

"Of course," he replies in his normal voice. I then hear the bell over the door ding and watch as some kids from school file in. There is Bridgett, Samantha, and Willow (all cheerleaders that have never been particularly nice to me unless Grace was around), followed by Mitchell and Parker. Both of the guys play football and run track so they say hello as they pass and take a seat a few booths behind ours. Suddenly, Luca jumps up and says "Let's play a game. You name the track for the jukebox and if I can guess which song it is, you have to kiss me right here and right now."

"Well my, sir. I feel this first date is moving a little too fast for me and I beg to be pardoned." I use my best British accent but Luca staring intensely across the table at me leaves me breathless.

"Trust me on this. Okay, so take these two quarters and go pick." I take the change from his hand and make my way over to the juke box. I try to find a good one that will hopefully throw him off his game.

"F3."

"Seriously? That is all you got?" he says with a smile that sends my heart racing. "'Can't help falling in love with you' by Elvis."

My jaw drops to the ground as the song starts to play. Is this part of his heightened senses? Can he read the jukebox from our table?

"How'd you do that?" I ask in wonder as he makes his way over to me.

"A magician never shares his secrets, now does he? Where would the fun be in that?" He takes my hand and then wraps the other around my waist, pulling me closer. "May I have this dance?"

"Here? In the middle of the diner?" I can't tell if I am embarrassed to think that the kids from school would make fun of us or I am really flattered by the romantic gesture. I decide it is the latter. "I'd love to."

Luca pulls me in as all the noise fades out with the exception of Elvis's voice. The melody wrapping around me like a warm comforting blanket. He doesn't realize that I chose this song because my dad used to sing it to my mom as they danced around the kitchen. The irony isn't lost on me. I look over Luca's shoulder and can see that we've definitely drawn the attention of the one other table in the restaurant. Bridgett and Samantha's mouths are so wide they could catch flies and their eyes are the size of saucers. I smile to myself and bury my head in Luca's shoulders.

The song comes to an end as Luca elegantly dips me back and stares into my eyes before raising me back up. He bends down until our noses are touching and tells me, "My mom made me take ballroom dancing for a few years. I should've warned you." Then I feel his lips gingerly graze mine before I feel the soft and pleasant pressure of his mouth. I suddenly hear the bacon on the griddle sizzling, the hushed whispers of the other table, Rosie is smacking her gum somewhere, and the neon light in the window is crackling and buzzing.

As we pull away and I gaze up at him, I notice that the kids from school are exiting. I hear Bridgett call over her shoulder, "I've lost my appetite. Let's just go grab a Starbucks." I feel my cheeks flush over the realization that she is referring to our dance and kiss. I am not used to showing public displays of affection and would normally be mortified but when I look up to see Luca's grin, I feel a bubble of laughter welling up inside of me. I can't help it and now I am doubled over with tears streaking down my face.

"What is so funny?" He asks with the same grin, a grin that says he just got away with murder, plastered all over his face.

"It is just that this is the first time in almost a week that I have felt like a normal kid. I wish that Grace was here to witness this whole scene. She never would believe I danced AND kissed you in public." Luca takes my hand and leads me back to the booth. As we take our seats, Rosie returns with our food.

"Oh you two kids are just adorable. Makes my old heart so happy to see you so happy, Gemma. Enjoy!" As Rosie disappears, I look at Luca.

He is still smiling, and I have to ask, "What was that all about anyway? What has you so happy? You're normally more sultry than this." I have to break eye contact and act like I am busying myself pouring syrup on my pancakes.

"First off. Nobody could be sultry when they woke up in your room and held you as you slept. Second off. I am smiling because when those girls came in and sat down, one of them said to the other that you and I must be cousins because there is no way that you and I would be together. Apparently you have a prudish reputation. Then one of the guys told the other guy that you were hot. So I had to prove one of them wrong and the other right." He shrugs and then begins to smother his eggs in hot sauce.

"Am I just a game to you, Luca?" I hate the way I sound like that girl when I ask him but he seems so satisfied with himself that he made one of the girls, probably Bridgett, eat her words and it is like he claimed his territory all at once. I am intrigued to know that one of the guys found me attractive, but it doesn't matter because the feelings I am developing for Luca are the most real thing I have ever felt. I am almost afraid of what his answer is going to be. I watch as he finishes chewing and swallows.

"That is the last thing you are to me. I can tell you when that kid said you were hot, I felt a jealousy that I hadn't ever felt. When that girl doubted that we could be an item, I felt protective over you. Like how can she not see all the great things you are and how breathtaking you are? So to answer your question, you are not even close to a game. I am sorry if that is how you felt." Now I do feel really stupid. I look down at my food and feel a smile tugging at the corners of my mouth.

"What?" He is mid bite into a piece of toast that he has covered in strawberry jelly.

"Nothing. I just can't believe you'd be jealous. Over me."

"I'd be stupid not to be."

The rest of the meal seems to fly by. We talked about how he used to surf with sharks in Cocoa Beach, that he surprisingly has read a book by Nicholas Sparks, he used to dream of being an artist and loved works by Picasso, that he is extremely close to his mom, and when he was little, he met John Glenn at the Space Center (definitely one of his prouder moments). I shared that I have always wanted to parachute but I am afraid of heights, I used to want a pet pig until my dad told me their life expectancy so I settled for a guinea pig, I don't care much for jewelry but I love rubies, and my dream travel destination is anywhere in the Caribbean so I can see the crystal blue waters. When I glance back at the time, we have been in here for almost three hours and it is creeping up on twelve thirty.

We stand to leave and as we are paying our check at the counter, the bells over the door ring. I turn and find my dad shuffling in with a tall, leggy, blonde. He has his hand on the small of her back and they are laughing about something. She places her hand on his chest and I see a blush creep across his cheeks. Once they have made their way through the door, he reaches down and takes her hand in his. All this time, he hasn't even realized that I am standing right in front of him observing his every move.

Luca has finished up with Rosie and turns around smacking right into me. My feet feel cemented to the floor. He puts his arm around my shoulders and tries to lead me to the exit when he looks up and realizes why I am transfixed in this spot. He looks back to me and that is when my dad also takes notice that we happen to be standing in the same restaurant only a few feet from one another. He drops her hand immediately and she looks to me.

I take her in. Her big blue eyes, flawless skin, plump red lips… she is absolutely beautiful and her hand was just on my dad's chest. She is tall and thin, probably somewhere around my dad's age, she looks back to him.

Sensing the discomfort, Luca intervenes.

"Mr. Jacobs. Such a pleasure to see you again." He extends his hand in my dad's direction and seems to snap my dad out of whatever reverie he was just in.

"Yes, Luca. Pleasure is all mine. Glad to see you two kids are out making the most of the day." He looks nervously to me and back to Luca. "Abigail, this is my daughter Gemma."

"Gemma. I have heard so much about you." I can see her mouth moving but I don't know how to respond. It is like being in an alternate universe. My body is here but I feel numb and tingly all over. At this point, everyone is staring at me waiting for me to respond but I can't find the words. I feel a hand on my lower back and realize it is Luca. His touch alone jolts me out of my trance as I take in a deep steadying breath.

"Hi, Abigail. I hope you two enjoy your lunch." Without so much as a second glance toward my dad, I lead Luca out the door and make my way to the car. I hear the door to the diner swing open as I am opening the passenger door and my dad is calling my name but I don't care. Seems like we are keeping a lot of important things from one another these days and I just need to put as much space between us and him as I can. All my life he has preached honesty to me and now, he can't even practice what he preaches. I can feel the heat rolling off me in waves.

As if Luca can sense this, he backs out of our spot and we are turning onto the highway heading toward the lake.

Chapter 7

We ride in silence most of the way to our spot. There is something comfortable about not having to talk to Luca. He has his hand on my thigh and is rubbing little circles with this thumb while the other hand is tapping along to the beat on his steering wheel. Today's road trip music is David Bowie and I have to admit that I am impressed.

We arrive at our spot and he jumps out carrying a bag that I instantly recognize my bikini strap hanging out of. He walks around to the trunk and pulls out a small cooler.

"What's this?" I ask as he saunters over to where I am standing, mouth agape, and hands on my hips.

"I told you. You're going to spend the day being a normal teenager."

"What I meant was how did you get my bikini out of my bedroom without me noticing and have you stolen anything else?"

Luca's face turns read and his face breaks out into the sheepish grin that stirs something inside of me that I haven't felt before.

"Okay, so when I was hiding from your dad in your closet, I saw it sitting on the shelf and thought to grab it so we could spend the day down here. But I have also managed to sneak out *Twilight*." I can't help it and I break out into a fit of laughter. Here is this boy that I just met, that I trust with my life, that makes me feel more alive than I have since my mom left, and he is sneaking out my teen girl fiction novels and bikini.

I reach for the bikini and look around the wooded area that stands between us and the shoreline.

"You stay here. NO PEEKING!" Luca puts up two fingers, scout's honor, and crosses his heart. I scurry off to the trees and find a large trunk to hide behind as I change into my bathing suit. I feel breathless and excited, nervous and giddy at the thought of Luca's eyes on me. I feel a heat creep up my chest and spread into my neck at the thought of his fingertips grazing my skin. The images popping up in my mind are making me breathless. I tie the bikini behind my neck and look down evaluating myself.

I have strong slender legs and a flat stomach from the years I have spent running. I used to feel boyish in comparison to Grace who was curvier in the right ways while I was taller, thinner, and more angular than she was, but I have grown to appreciate my body. I just hope that Luca does the same.

I go to step around the tree to call out to Luca but as I turn around, I run right into him. I try not to worry about how long he has been standing there, what he may have seen, and the possibility of him seeing me feeling as flustered as I was. My eyes trail up his exposed chest that is chiseled like he does nothing but pushups and bench press in his spare time, to his shoulders that have the muscular curvature of a Greek God, to his angular jaw and shining blue eyes that are drinking me in. I never knew that he was so strong. Sure, I could feel he was solid, but I didn't think he was solid as an oak tree.

Our eyes are locked and his hands start trailing a path from my wrists all the way up my arms leaving goosebumps in their wake. My heart is hammering in my chest as his fingers leave my shoulders and start trailing their way up my neck, slowly, torturing me. Standing rooted in this spot and not pulling him to me is taking all the strength that I have. His hands are cupped around my neck and jaw as he pulls my face closer to his. Right as our lips are about to meet, he pauses resting his forehead against mine. I dare to look at him and see that his eyes are closed, lost in this moment that feels like it is only ours. The concern of being watched and followed seems like a distant worry compared to how we are feeling here and now.

I put my arms around his waist and start running my fingers gently up his back as a soft moan escapes his lips. I am so new to this, to feeling so empowered as a woman and daring, but it all comes so naturally with Luca. I never question, "Is this right? Is this how I should respond?" I can't wait any longer and I tilt my head so that I can feel the soft, yet firmness, of his lips on mine.

His kiss is tentative at first and his hands cradle me like I am a fragile doll that he is afraid to break. I open my mouth as an invitation to him. His mouth gives way to me, and he spins me around so that my back is pressed up against the tree. As we kiss, I can feel the rough bark of the tree pressing into my skin, biting at it like little razor blades but I don't care. I can hear the bird building its nest fifteen feet above us. I can smell the moisture in the air that assures me that there is rain on the way. But through all this sensory overload, I can feel Luca's weight pushed against me, his hands on my hips as he pulls me toward him, and my hands around his neck fisting in his hair. The butterflies in my chest take flight and I throw caution to the wind. His hands reach for my butt, lifting me up, and I wrap my legs around him pulling him closer. No amount of closeness will feel close enough right now.

He stops kissing me and starts hungrily trailing his lips down my neck. I toss my head back reveling in this feeling. While I am completely perplexed as to why it took me eighteen years to experience this, I am grateful that it is with Luca and how comfortable he is making me feel. I pull his hair in response to the shivers he sent down my spine and hear his breathing grow husky. I feel his lips break into a smile against my skin as he goes back to kiss the sensitive spot just below my ear and he garners the same reaction.

I can tell that he is very pleased with himself. I reach for his face pulling his mouth back to mine. We are both hungry for more. He pulls my bottom lip with his teeth, and I feel like I am about to come unglued but then he stops and sets me down, taking a few steps back but keeping his hands on my hips. His breath is coming quick, and I can tell that stopping wasn't his ideal plan, but he has enough restraint to take a step back. That makes one of us.

"I just... I know that... I know that this is all new for you, Gemma." I feel myself blush. "I am enjoying kissing you and feeling you way too much. I don't want this to escalate to a step that you aren't ready for." I let his words sink in. Was that really where we were heading? I feel a pinching in my stomach and realize that is EXACTLY where this was heading. I take a few breaths as he looks at me waiting for a response. I see uncertainty in his eyes.

"I am ready, Luca. I see what all the hype is about, and I just really want to take this further with you." I think about it and in the week that I have known him, he has brought me to life. It is like I hadn't taken a breath until him. That scares me because of the three people that have ever meant a great deal to me, one is lying to me, one left me, and one died. This magnetic pull I feel toward him is so new.

"I am glad you feel that way and I want to be the one you experience these things with, but I'd prefer to do it in a way that you are worthy of. Not out in the open. You deserve all the firsts of your life to be memorable. I want to give you that." He steps toward me and places his palm against my cheek. I lean into it and close my eyes, inhaling the scent of his cologne and the woods around us. I forever want to remember this moment with him where he looked at me like I hung the stars in the sky. Nobody has ever looked at me like that.

"What do you say we just head down to the water and cool off? Literally." He smiles that smile that I now look to for comfort and takes my hand in his leading the way.

We lay by the shore with a Bluetooth speaker playing 80s music. Jessie's Girl is streaming through the speakers, there is a bag of Doritos and two pops between us (or as Luca calls them, two sodas). The lake is relatively quiet but the day is beautiful, though I see some rain clouds out in the distance threatening to disturb our good time. It is, after all, the rainy season here at home. Afternoon thunderstorms aren't uncommon.

Luca managed to shove one of my books in the bag on his way out this morning so I am doing a little reading and watching him breeze through the pages of *Twilight*. I should go ahead and get *New Moon* ready for him because it won't be long before he has moved on to the next.

I am looking at him and he smirks, the left corner of his mouth turning up.

"What are you thinking about?"

"Honestly? I was just thinking about how different my life was just a week ago... and I was wondering if you managed to grab any more snacks."

"Want to leave and go grab some lunch?" I shake my head. No I am not ready to head back into town. Town is where my problems with my dad are waiting for me, and I am not ready to face those yet. Luca has tried to talk to me about it a few times, but I refuse to budge. I don't want to discuss him and what he may potentially be hiding from me. Last I checked, he and my mom weren't even divorced. I guess you'd have to know where she is in order to serve her the papers though. Is a divorce what he would want or does he still hold out hope that she will return? All this time I thought he was fragile and still pining for my mom but Abigail seems to tell a different story.

"Don't forget that we are going to the Alliance tonight. Demora will be waiting to see what you've got." And like that, his nose is back in the book. With all the trouble we had this morning with Adams and Hughes, followed by the diner drama with my dad and Abigail, I had completely forgotten about telling Demora I would be present tonight at the Alliance. It seems like such a big deal and I am not prepared.

"Can you practice that exercise with me that Demora and I did together?" We had said we wouldn't discuss anything about the Alliance or abilities today, other than the reminder that I was already booked for the evening. Luca hesitates before he sits up and instructs me to close my eyes and clear my mind. He then tells me he wants me to imagine my perfect vacation. What a perfect topic seeing as how I would rather be anywhere with him than here where the SGP and my dad are all waiting for me.

I close my eyes, take a deep breath in, and I picture the beach in Jamaica. I used to look at pictures on my computer at school just waiting for the day when I could go see the crystal-clear waters, so blue that they melt into the sky. I can feel the ocean mist splashing me on the face, the sun warming my body, and somewhere in the distance, I can smell the jerk seasonings from a roadside hut selling chicken. The sand beneath us is soft and inviting, like powder, lining the shore. Luca is beside me with an umbrella drink in his hand and we can hear the sound of steel drums playing quietly as if creating the utmost perfect background noise. On one side we have the beach but there are mountains behind us and the atmosphere is charged between us but we feel an inner peace, just completely relaxed in each other's company.

"Woah. Okay, Gemma. Keep picturing it and focus on projecting it out. And on the count of three, I want you to open your eyes. One... two... three!" As Luca commanded, I snap my eyes open and I immediately catch my breath. The lake's water is translucent and shimmering in the sunlight. The steel drums are a little louder and, as I look around, I realize I am in the image I was creating. The drums echo through the mountains and over to the right, opposite of the beach, there is smoke floating and carrying the smell of the jerk seasonings.

"This is remarkable," I manage to stammer out, "it feels like we are really there." Luca looks at me with eyes full of wonder, eyes that tell me he is as mesmerized as I feel, as he reaches out and cups the right side of my face.

"You, Gemma Jacobs, are truly remarkable." He presses his lips to mine in an intimate kiss. Suddenly, the waves are lapping on the beach. The ocean mist is spraying onto our bodies and glistening on our sun-kissed skin. I can feel the sand giving way beneath us as we move closer together until we are touching. The sun is radiating its warmth over us and I can feel it sticking to my skin. I marvel at the feel of his lips, smooth and firm. I concentrate on the feel of his hand, strong and soft. I can hear every breath he takes as if I am breathing it into my own lungs.

He shifts his weight until he is laying over me, body positioned between my legs and his hand trailing up my thigh and coming to a rest on my hip. He nips at my bottom lip and I can't believe that I am wrapping my legs around his waist. His breath is hot against my neck but I remember the self-control he had earlier and put my palms against his chest.

"Maybe we should go for a swim and cool off... literally." He laughs against my skin at my use of his own words against him and tucks his head between my breasts.

"Fine but only if you let me carry you down there because it is detrimental to my health that I am touching you." My heart stammers as he stands up and reaches down to pull me to my feet, our Jamaican scene falling away. I wrap my arms around his neck and feel his hands reach behind my thighs and hoist me up around his waist.

As he walks into the water, a shriek escapes my lips and goosebumps cover his skin.

"Holy shit this water is colder than I expected," he says, laughing but still plowing on straight into the water. The stillness of it is a sharp contrast to my beating heart. It tickles my ankles and then, before I know it, we are up to my chest deep.

"Please, whatever you do, don't get my hair wet. I really don't want to have to fool with it before tonight." The words leave my mouth and I instantly know that it is a mistake. The mischievous glint in his eye tells me that I am really in for it.

"So you'd probably be really upset if I were to, oh I don't know, do something like this?" Luca dunks us straight under the water as I protest and then springs us back to the surface. His laughter fills the air and echoes back to us.

"I CAN NOT BELIEVE YOU JUST DID THAT! You are so dead." As we both throw our heads back in laughter, I can't help but watch the water glistening on his sun-kissed skin, the freckles across his broad shoulders, and the way the water drips out of his hair and down into his face. He is so beautiful that I can't even feign anger.

He is still laughing as I lace my fingers behind his head and pull his face to meet mine. Our lips touch and he pulls me in closer so that our skin is flush together, two bodies so perfectly molded that it is like we are one. He tastes sweet from the coke he drank, his lips are wet, and I marvel at how I feel no matter how close I get, I am never close enough. I could get lost in him. It is both exhilarating and scary to feel so drawn to him with as little as I know about him. I trail my fingers down his spine and wrap my arms around his back. He is so strong and solid. I can feel every muscle in his back. The kiss is passionate but also full of lust and I can tell that he is as into me as I am into him.

I can smell the storm rolling in. I can hear the electric charge of the incoming clouds and I can't tell if the electricity is from the havoc they are threatening to spill out or if it is from us. Our moment is interrupted, the kiss is broken, as the thunder booms in the distance. As Luca pulls away, he looks at me with what I can only assume is adoration. There is a certain sincerity in his eyes and I realize I could get used to having him look at me this way.

"We better get going so we don't get caught in the rain. Want to come back to my place before The Alliance meeting or do you want me to take you home?" Going home with Luca sounds like a really enticing idea. Home is such a weird word to me right now. Home used to mean honesty and happiness. It meant finding peace and tranquility when you walked over the threshold but I don't feel those things any more, at least not right now. I feel it is full of lies and deceit, lies about my mom, lies about my dad's dating life. It is empty without the possibility of Grace ever coming through the door again. It lacks safety after seeing how easily Hughes and Adams can appear. Luca is looking at me waiting for an answer to his question.

"Can we go by my place so I can grab a few things and then head back to yours? I don't want to run the risk of having to talk to my dad yet. I just need a little more time to process everything."

He nods at me and stands to collect our things, throwing his bag over his shoulder before offering me his hand. I take it and he pulls me to my feet before placing a kiss on my forehead. "Whatever you'd like, princess. Your wish is my command."

We pull into my driveway and I am instantly filled with dread. I worry that I will walk in to find Hughes and Adams waiting for me in the kitchen like we are going to have a friendly chat over a meat and cheese tray. I worry that I will go in and Abigail will be hanging pictures of her and my dad, replacing the ones that have hung on those walls since I can remember. I know these are all irrational fears but they are there nonetheless.

"Do you hear anything? Is the house empty?" I look to Luca asking him to use his abilities to let me know what I am walking into.

"It sounds like either your dad is here or you forgot to turn the TV off. I can go in with you and check if you'd like but I don't feel that Hughes and Adams are inside. That is, unless they've managed to slip by me again. Not like those two do a whole lot of talking anyways… I imagine they communicate with each other with head nods and different variations of grunts." I can't help but laugh picturing those two ever having a conversation.

"I'd love for you to come in. Maybe then if my dad is home, you can be a buffer or he won't want to discuss anything too heavy with company over." I open the car door and slide out of the seat. I pause by the gardenia bush as I make my way up the steps, inhaling deep and closing my eyes to try and calm my nerves. Luca reaches for my hand and gives it a reassuring squeeze before I walk in the door.

I don't see my dad at first but I do hear the TV. Sounds like he is watching reruns of *Law and Order* again. We certainly love our crime shows in this family and I smirk thinking about the way Luca was so abrupt when I mentioned ending up on an episode of *Dateline*.

"Just wait right here and I will be right back. I just want to grab a few things so I can shower and change at your place." I stand on my toes and plant a kiss on his cheek before darting up the stairs as quietly as possible.

As I open my bedroom door, I can hear my dad downstairs say, "Well if it isn't Luca the triangle player standing in my foyer? You don't really play the triangle, do you?" I realize this is my cue to pick up the pace and pack my bag before anything unfolds downstairs that I won't be happy about. I don't want to risk embarrassing secrets spilled or a possible interrogation.

Tossing my hairbrush, travel bag with my hair products and toothbrush, and a change of clothes into my backpack, I run down the stairs at full speed praying with every step that I don't tumble down. When I enter the room, I can hear they are talking about Florida and I am instantly at ease. Nothing can go wrong there.

"Gemma. I was hoping that we could talk. In private if that is all right?" My dad is looking at me with these big Bambi eyes that make me feel guilty but I am in no mood to discuss anything with him right now. I have every right to feel angry with him and he can't tell me otherwise. At this point, I don't see a conversation being productive and I really don't want to have this discussion where I know Luca can hear it no matter where it is that he is standing in the house, or in the driveway for that matter.

"You know, Dad, I don't feel like talking yet. See you tonight." I turn toward the door that Luca is already opening for me but my dad is talking again.

"Where are you going? Why can't we talk? We have always talked, you and me. Come on, Gemma. Just a few minutes." Something inside me snaps because I feel my face flush with anger. I spin around on him and see the concern in his eyes but I don't feel the guilt any more. The guilt has been replaced with fury at the fact that he is making me feel like this is my fault. I try my best to take a few deep breaths before responding and I try to keep the edge out of my voice.

"You know what is funny about that, Dad? I always thought we talked too. I always thought that we were honest with one another, no secrets. Then I find out that Mom had abilities that nobody felt it was necessary to tell me about. You brought a new woman into your life and didn't think to tell me. You said she was a client but judging by the way you two seemed so comfortable with each other at Tiffany's, she is definitely more than a client." I see my dad flinch at these comments and the concern is replaced with sadness but I am not finished yet. "It seems very unfair to me that Abigail knew who I was, had heard so much about me, yet I didn't even know that she existed. Now, I said I don't feel like talking yet. I am going to Luca's to hang out and will be home before curfew. And while we are being honest, Luca does not play the triangle, we don't go to school together, and I really like him. See you tonight."

I wipe at the tears in my eyes that I hadn't even realized were betraying me and I stride out the front door. As I walk past Luca, I can see that his eyes are wide. He pulls the door shut behind him and scurries to my side of the car to open the car door for me. He slides into the driver's seat and, after we are heading down my street, he reaches for my hand. We ride all the way to his house in silence while he traces circular patterns on the back of my hand with his thumb.

Chapter 8

Luca's mom isn't home when we arrive. She apparently left early to go to The Alliance and get some paperwork done or something along those lines. I am not really listening to Luca when he gives me an explanation because I can't hear anything over my stomach growling. He seems to be able to sense how hungry I am and heads straight into the kitchen opening cabinets and the fridge as he goes.

"We have a couple hours before we need to leave so what can I get you? I make a mean PB&J but you may be too classy for that." He looks to me with a container of Peter Pan Creamy Peanut Butter in his hand and I instantly smile. It is the same stuff that my dad always swore by. There was never another brand allowed in our home.

"Actually, that would be great. On one condition... do you have strawberry jelly?" Luca's smile brightens as he walks to the fridge again pulling out the strawberry jelly and getting to work on my sandwich. He makes two, one for each of us, cuts them diagonally, and puts fresh fruit on the plate. Who knew that he was such a thoughtful host? We practically swallow the sandwiches whole, not realizing how hungry we really were, and then he walks me to his bathroom to get me set up for a shower.

He is adjusting the water temperature while I stand leaning in the doorway with my arms crossed. I can't help but admire his long arms, his toned physique, and the way his waist is smaller than his broad shoulders. I always thought the swimmers in school had the best bodies. Apparently, that goes for surfers too. Once he is satisfied, he turns and catches me looking. I bite my bottom lip to hide the fact that I have just been caught checking him out. Luca blushes and rubs the back of his neck, a sign that he is nervous, and makes his way toward me.

"I placed a towel for you over the hook by the shower and the water should be perfect. It can be a little temperamental so if you need any help, just holler for me. I nod in acknowledgement and look down, dragging my foot back and forth on the cold white marble tile of the bathroom. I can sense he is still looking at me so I look up to meet his gaze.

"Earlier, at your house, you told your dad that you really like me. Is that a true statement?" My heart starts beating so hard that it feels like a battering ram to my rib cage. I have to look away. I am so embarrassed. I had completely forgot that I threw that out there before marching out of the house. I force myself to look back into Luca's blue eyes, so blue that they remind me of the Jamaican waters from earlier.

"Yeah. So, what if uh – so what if it is true?" I am trying to sound confident but I can feel the butterflies in my stomach threatening to break loose. He takes a sharp breath in and licks his lips. The silence seems to stretch on for what feels like forever.

"Well if it is true, then I would have to say that I really like you too. Like I have never liked anyone before to be straight up with you. I like you so much that it scares me how much you've grown to mean to me in the span of just a week." I quickly close the one foot of space between us and throw my arms around his neck, pulling his face down to meet mine. Once our lips are touching, I can smell every scent of soap in this bathroom. I can hear the water as it runs down the drain, many feet below us into the ground. I can feel the heat coming off of the water. It still amazes me that every time we kiss, my senses are heightened. This must be what it feels like to be him.

Luca's hands find my waist and pull me in to him. I can feel his excitement pressing between my legs and the desire for him is so strong that I can't think about anything else. His hands then trail up under my shirt while I wrap my hands in his hair. His mouth is on my neck kissing a trail from my jaw to my collarbone and then I feel his hands cupping my breasts and his thumbs circle my nipples making it hard for me to breathe. I let out a groan and feel a pressure building up in my stomach that is so new to me that I marvel at its intensity. He slides off my shirt and takes my nipple in his mouth while his thumb continues to tease the other one.

I am practically frozen in place reveling in this feeling. As he takes my other nipple now between his teeth, I feel like my knees might give out. He begins kissing down my stomach now leaving no inch untouched and when he reaches the top of my pants, he begins to run his tongue across my skin just above the waistband. My breath is becoming more and more ragged and all I want is for this pressure to be released. He unbuttons and removes my shorts to find that I am still wearing my bathing suit bottoms from earlier. He looks up at me through his long lashes, the want and desire evident on his face, and his eyes ask for permission to continue.

Rather than say anything and ruin this moment, I hook my thumbs into the top of my bottoms and start easing them down, slowly, watching him and awaiting his reaction. I feel self-conscious for a split second before I realize he is looking me over appreciatively. He starts to lightly trace his fingers from my thighs up. Standing, he presses his mouth to mine and our kiss is hungry, aggressive in a sense, like we can't get enough of each other. This is our oxygen and if we don't get enough, we might suffocate. I want to suffocate in him, wrapped up in this euphoria.

Without breaking our kiss, Luca picks me up and I wrap my legs around his waist. The hardness in his pants now pressing into me perfectly, making me want him more. I move my hips so I am grinding against him and I feel a shiver run over his body and he groans against my mouth. He starts making his way to the shower and, though he is still fully dressed, he climbs in the running water, drenching us both. The warm water doesn't deter me and only turns me on more. Luca presses me up against the cold tile wall, the contrast creating goosebumps across my skin. With his hands holding under my butt and his mouth now on my neck, I reach for him and take him in my hand through his pants, stroking him as best I can from this angle, but he quickly stops me and sets me down gently. I open my eyes and look into his, hoping that the silent plea to continue is evident. He runs his fingers across my breasts, down my stomach until he is teasingly running them right below my waist line. I grab his hand and ease it down lower until it comes to a rest between my legs, cupping me in a way that makes my heart race even faster. I want him to know that this is okay, that I am okay, that I am ready for us to take another step.

Slowly he slides his fingers in me and though it hurts at first, after a few strokes, I feel a fire ignite in my body and spread to every limb. His mouth is on mine, his other hand encircling my waist, his pace picking up. I have one hand holding the back of his head and the other helping his hand thrust back and forth. I've never been touched before. I never thought that it would feel this good to be intimate with someone you care about. My breathing is coming fast and I feel like I am gasping for air. His mouth moves to my neck and I am pressing against his hand, practically begging him for more.

He pulls his face back just enough to rest his forehead against mine and stares into my eyes. I am finding it hard to maintain eye contact, feeling sheepish and shy under his glare. I can feel myself coming undone. He whispers in my ear, his warm breath sending shivers down my spine. "Do you like this, Gemma? Or do you prefer this?"

He slows down his pace and begins to twist his fingers inside me and I feel it coming. I can't help the moan that escapes my lips as he whispers again, "I think I found my answer." And then I come, his name falling from my lips. I feel every muscle in my body contracting and it feels like my blood is rushing to my head. He quiets my moans with his mouth, my legs shaking, as he sucks on my bottom lip.

He pulls me close, steadying me with my head against his chest and his arms supporting me while I try to catch my breath. The water is beating against his back, steam billowing all around us. He puts his hand under my chin and tilts my face up to meet his, planting a small kiss on my lips. When I am able to look into his eyes, I see the adoration there again and my heart swells. I still haven't wrapped my head around the fact that we are standing in the shower together and he just gave me my first real orgasm. I feel like I am floating and watching someone else living these experiences because the Gemma that I was a week ago wouldn't have done this.

"Thank you." I look up at Luca, not sure that I heard him correctly. Thank you? Who says that?

"You… are welcome? Why are you thanking me?" I ask, my voice barely above a whisper.

"Because you just shared a very intimate thing with me and

I feel honored that you felt comfortable enough to be vulnerable with me. It was so sexy." I feel a flush creep over my whole body as I take in his words.

"You are the first person I have ever been intimate with. So thank you for being someone that I feel I can trust." I look deep into his eyes and see the warmth that he has there. I can't believe that this is the same guy that I met just a week ago, the guy that I thought was arrogant, and the guy that I was convinced would abduct me. He is standing here, more like we are standing here, in his shower, and I feel my heart might burst from pure joy. Part of me feels guilty for being so giddy when Grace isn't here to share it with me and I can feel my smile fall a little bit.

"Are you all right?" It amazes me how easily he can already pick up on my mood shifts and sees the turmoil building within me. I suddenly feel so exhausted.

"Yeah, I just feel tired now. Could really go for a nap. It has been such a long, and very enjoyable, day." I smile at him now and note the way his hands wrap around my waist and pull me into him. He makes me feel so safe and secure here with him and all the other worries in the world just fade away.

Luca turns and steps out of the shower grabbing the sky-blue towel from the hook by the shower door and begins to towel his head. He pulls his shirt off and then slips out of his pants, leaving his boxers on but they don't leave much to the imagination. I feel guilty again. This time it isn't about enjoying life while my best friend's was cut short but it is because I got to have this pleasurable experience and Luca didn't get it reciprocated. He turns to look at me with the towel around his waist and a smile playing at his lips. Bending over, he grabs a towel from a basket on the floor and then turns the water off. He lifts the towel and begins to dry my hair and then continues down my body drying every inch of me. When he gets between my legs, I can still feel the throbbing sensation and he must know that it is super sensitive because he is gentle and careful before continuing all the way down my legs. I watch him the entire time and marvel at the way his muscles in his back and shoulder blades contract as he dries each leg and then comes up to wrap the towel around me. He plants a kiss at my temple and places his forehead against mine. I figure this is my chance to even the score.

I reach down and place my hand around him and hear his sharp intake of breath. He places his hand over mine and lets out a sigh.

"Gemma, you don't have to do that."

"I know but I want to. I shouldn't get to have all the fun."

"You think that I didn't just enjoy unraveling the girl that I like in the shower? You think that wasn't fun for me because despite what you may have heard, that is fulfilling for me too. I just want this moment to be about you. There is plenty of time for everything else." I am relieved that Luca doesn't want anything from me. Not because I am not willing to give it to him but because I am so nervous about being bad at something. I know he has to have been with other girls and I have no experience so what if I don't measure up to them?

He takes my hand and leads me into his room. I fetch my clothes from my bag and start to dress while Luca gets changed behind me. I was tempted to steal a glance at him but I am afraid of getting caught so I check my phone instead and see that I have two missed calls from my dad and a text from him asking if we can talk this evening when I get home. I sigh and realize that we still have a couple hours before we need to meet Demora. I turn to find Luca is now sprawled on his bed laying on his back with an arm behind his head. Eyes are closed but I know he isn't sleeping so I crawl in beside him placing my head on his chest and start tracing circles across the top of his solid black V-neck he has slipped on. I feel my eyes are getting heavy and rather than fighting it, I let sleep take me over. Despite my dad and his... girlfriend? I still feel content and happy as I drift off to sleep.

After Luca wakes me, I run a brush through my hair, and I slip into my Converse before we are on our way to The Alliance. I am so nervous and excited but have no idea what I should expect. Will there be a lot of people? Will these people think I am strange or will I feel more welcome because we all have abilities? Do they all know my mom? All my questions are whizzing through my head while Luca drives, one hand on the wheel and the other on my thigh drumming along to the musical notes of Journey. When he pulls up outside tall steel gates and a brick wall that is overgrown with vines, I feel a shiver run down my spine.

    I look around as the security guard lets us pass and notice that it is in fact an old state hospital. I had heard about this place in school. It used to be a lunatic asylum and only closed about fifteen years ago. They used to treat patients with all sorts of disorders, ranging from women with PMS to murderers. All my visions of an old hospital run through my mind and I am afraid to walk in and see the same hospital beds, fluorescent lights, and green walls. That takes those visions from being something of my nightmares to being a real possibility and I can't stomach that. I can't bear the thought of Luca being tied up and at the mercy of Hughes and Adams or whoever that Elijah was. I grab his hand and he gives mine a reassuring squeeze before interlacing his fingers with mine.

    I take in the lush green landscape with all the large mossy trees hanging over the drive leading to the back of the property.

The grounds are large and sprawling with a lot of shade and, off in the distance, I spot the building. There is a small pond on the right as we make our way up the path and I notice a few people with blankets sitting by the edge socializing. There are a few more stragglers walking together through the trees along the edge of the road. They give us a wave as we pass by but everyone looks so… normal? Not sure why I was expecting the sort of things you see in an X-Men movie or out of a circus.

"I thought this place burned down years ago?" My mouth is agape in amazement.

"That is what we wanted people to think. To the naked eye, you wouldn't see this place as you drove by the grounds. There is someone within The Alliance that shields it from outsiders. You can only see it if you've been invited in by one of the board members." Then he swings into a parking space and I realize we have made it to our destination. Luca jumps out and I try to take a few calming breaths before making my exit but, before I can open the door, there he is extending a hand and helping me out. When I am standing, he doesn't retract my hand and instead heads toward the steps leading inside. At the top of the stairs is Demora and Darcy. Demora is relaxed with her hair hanging loosely to her waist and a light flowing sundress that falls to her ankles. Darcy has a playful smirk on her face as she looks down to our hands and then back up between the two of us. My face flushes out of embarrassment. I haven't ever had a boyfriend, held hands in public, and now here I am holding hands with a boy that I don't know if he is my boyfriend as we stand in front of his mom. I feel that our activities of the day are written all over my face.

When we make it to the top, Demora doesn't at all seem surprised and instead plants a kiss on each of my cheeks before throwing her arms around me.

"Welcome, Gemma. My goodness we are so pleased you could make it. Thank you for coming by." When she releases me, Darcy pulls me into a hug and then holds me at arm's length, hands on my shoulders, and looks me in the eyes. I hold my breath expecting a lecture but she smiles a warm smile and I again feel surrounded by a motherly love.

"I can't wait to show you all the things that your mother poured into this place. It wouldn't be nearly as amazing if it weren't for her touch." Darcy is practically bursting at the seams with excitement.

"Darcy, you have GOT to learn to give yourself some credit my dear!" Demora reaches out and places a hand on Darcy's shoulder and then turns to Luca.

"Luca, my love, could you do me a large favor? While we show Gemma around, could you gather everyone in the arena?" Luca grips my hand a little tighter and looks to me for approval. He has his bottom lip between his teeth and I sense he is hesitating because he fears to leave my side. "You have our word that we won't let a thing happen to her, will we, Darcy?" I can tell Demora is teasing him so I smile and give him a slight head nod. He pulls me in and plants a kiss on my forehead before heading back down the stairs and out to the grounds. I watch him as he goes and feel a blush creep up my cheeks when I realize that Demora and Darcy are watching me watch him closely.

"Right this way, sweetheart." Demora beckons me to follow her as her and Darcy exchange knowing smiles. What is that about? Is it about me and Luca? Is it because I am finally here and roaming these halls like my mom used to? I can't tell but I hate feeling left out of what seems like a secret between the two of them.

As we walk into the foyer, I am startled by the beauty. These walls are nothing like the ones of my vision. They are painted a soft cream color with modern art on display. The old hospital floors have been replaced with white marble and there are plush, high-backed chairs with soft lit lamps between them. To my left is a large oak desk decorated with family picture frames and a computer. Suddenly, a girl appears behind it and gives me a brilliant smile. She has long dark hair that catches the light and gives off blue hues, freckles dot her cheeks and nose, her green eyes are almost cat like. She is almost my height and wearing a black blazer with jeans and ballet flats which looks sophisticated enough to belong here. I suddenly feel very self-conscious of my jean shorts, white tank top, and red and white high topped Converse.

"This is Sasha. She is our executive assistant. She arranges all travel and meetings for the board members. Sasha, this is Gemma Jacobs." Demora places her hand on my shoulder and Sasha's gaze falls on me with wide wondering eyes. I can tell she's probably making the connection between me and my mom.

"So, this is the infamous Gemma that Luca has been spending so much time with?" I see that her cheeks are now flushed and realize it has nothing to do with my mom but with Luca... I make a mental note to ask him about her later.

"Yes, that is me! It is a pleasure to meet you." Then Darcy starts to lead us away down the long hallway. To my right there is a staircase that leads to the second floor. Its polished dark wood banister gleams in the lights and, as I am admiring the brilliance of this place, something catches my eye. There is a black and white canvas hanging on the wall by the stairs with four women standing with their arms around each other's shoulders. All of them are smiling like they were caught mid laugh and I am mesmerized by the happiness and strength in their eyes. As I approach it to get a better look, I see that Demora is all the way on the left, Darcy is beside her, there is a woman I don't recognize all the way to the right but there, third person from the left, stands my mother.

Her hair is cut to her shoulders just like she cut it before she left us. My whole life she had always had long hair so I know this had to be taken just before then. When she walked in the door that day after her hair appointment, Dad dropped his fork mid bite and my jaw almost landed into the middle of my algebra homework. We were in total shock as she walked in and ran her fingers through it nervously.

"Do you not like it? Is it too much?" she asked us. Dad went to her and weaved his fingers in it bringing her face to his and giving her a soft kiss. I was used to their displays of affection. They were always holding hands and stealing kisses when they didn't think I was looking.

He replied with, "Honey you could wear a garbage bag and still be the most beautiful thing in this world. If you love it, I love it." I feel a tear sliding down my cheek as I wonder where it all went wrong? What drove her away? Does Dad say those things to Abigail?

Darcy's arm is around me and startles me out of my trance. I feel like I have been cemented to this spot and nobody has said anything in what feels like several minutes.

"That was taken the day we got this place. We took it as soon as we opened the gates and stepped foot on the property. Your mom was so proud because the last place we had was burnt to the ground by the SGP. I remember she was so furious with them but she said nothing would squash our spirit and we would rebuild into bigger and better. She was absolutely right. She designed this place practically from top to bottom."

"I had no idea. Who is that on the right?" Darcy's voice drops to almost a whisper.

"That is Sasha's mom, Margo. She left just last year and nobody has heard from her, just like with your mom. Sasha has finally started smiling again but luckily for her, her mom had already helped her figure out her abilities and introduced her to us before taking off. I wish you had been able to say the same so we could have been there for you these last couple years but know we are here now."

"Yes, darling, you are family here. You are welcome any time." Demora is beside me now too and they then direct me back down the hallway. The first door we come to on the left is a library. It has bookshelves from floor to ceiling and even has one of those rolling ladders that I have only ever seen in *Beauty and the Beast*. There are a few tables with lights, a couple computers, more of the high-back chairs, thick area rugs with cushions on the floor, and there is a large window with a bench underneath that looks out on the grounds. There are a few people here, most have to be not much older than me. I am already excited to scour these shelves and spend time unwinding in here. A boy sitting cross legged on the floor with a large book looks up and gives a small wave before continuing with his reading and then we are back on our tour.

We pass bathrooms, a few vending machines tucked back in an alcove to the left, and then we come to a cafeteria on the right. The tables remind me of Hogwarts, long and wooden with benches down both sides. There is more of a family feel than anything to the community seating and I see on one wall there are tables set up with fruits, veggies, desserts, and quick grab and go snacks. On the opposite wall from the entry door there is a window and, from what I can see, a gourmet kitchen on the other side.

"The kitchen is open twenty-four hours a day, seven days a week, and can make almost anything you desire with a few exceptions. We service such a diverse group of people that we wanted to make sure all palettes were catered to. Rita is the main chef and she is often accompanied by Antonio and Marta. They are normally here from six a.m. to six p.m. and nights are covered by Joanna and Tyler." Surprisingly there isn't anyone in here around dinner time. But the tour continues and Darcy is leading the way.

"Here we have a clinic. It is open around the clock as well and free of charge. Everything we offer here is free to you. And right through those doors—" she gestures over her shoulder to a set of double doors "—you will find a full gym complete with a gymnasium and indoor swimming pool. But, from what I hear, you are more of a runner so I will make sure that Luca shows you the outdoor running trail." She smiles at me and looks up at Demora who has been quiet this whole time. Demora checks her watch and then gives us a brief nod.

"Ahh yes. It is time so I am afraid that is all the time we have right now. We have arranged for a group meeting so you can meet everyone." We start walking back toward the front door.

"Are we going to tour upstairs another time?" I can't help but ask. It feels like all the amenities this place could offer are right here on the first floor. What could possibly be up there?

"My dear, the top floor is filled with bedrooms. They are set like dorm rooms with a private bathroom and then community showers," Demora says, finally breaking her silence. I wasn't expecting this. I also can't help my mind from wandering to the shower that I took earlier and feel the heat creep up the back of my neck hoping that neither of them are mind readers.

"People actually live here? I thought this was just a safe meeting place." As we get closer to the front door, I see that people are starting to pour in and turn into a door across from the front desk. I hadn't noticed it there before as if it had appeared out of thin air. Demora picks up her pace and leaves us behind.

"It is but people also live here. Some people have powers they can't control yet or perhaps their friends and family aren't supportive. Others may even be hiding from the SGP. They all have their own stories but we let them decide how much of those stories they are willing to tell. We offer group therapy or private therapy sessions because if they lack a support system, they often lose themselves and let their abilities interfere with living their life to the fullest. This is when my ability to sense the power of others comes in handy. I can find them before they turn to things like self-harm or drugs and reassure them that they aren't alone and they aren't 'freaks'. We like to help people here in any way that we possibly can."

Luca just strolled through the door and my heart does a flutter. We lock eyes and the smile on his face could light the entire facility. As he makes his way over to us, not once breaking eye contact, I can also see out of the corner of my eye that Sasha is watching him walk in too. Darcy excuses herself as he makes his way over to me and disappears into the same room as everyone else.

He leans forward and places his lips on my forehead, murmuring against my skin, "I missed you." I look up into his eyes and give him a quick kiss before we can get caught by too many onlookers.

"Is that so? I wish you had been part of my tour." He wraps his arms around me and pulls me in so my head is against his chest and his chin rests on top of my head. I never thought that this would be my favorite place to be.

"No worries. I listened in the whole time just in case there was a moment that you needed rescuing. But now it is time to go to your first meeting and then I get you back all to myself." He drops his arm and takes my hand, leading me toward the mystery room but before we can make it through the doorway, he turns to whisper in my ear, "Oh, and by the way. I look forward to showing you every. Inch. Of that trail. Front and back. We can run fast or we can go slow. Not sure if you'd rather take your time... or race to the finish." His hot breath tickles my ear and I gulp in response. Instantly the knot has returned to my stomach and the desire for him is so strong that I would like to disappear into one of the bedrooms upstairs. I hear someone clear their throat and realize we are blocking the door. Sasha just gives us a look that I could only describe as disgust before squeezing past us. We both chuckle as Luca leads me through the doorway.

Chapter 9

The mystery room, or the arena as they call it, turns out to be the coziest place I have ever been. There is a fireplace on the far wall that has a small fire going, emitting a soft orange light. The floors went from marble to solid wood floors, like I noticed they had in the library, with more plush area rugs. There are four large couches that all face one another to create a circle so you can see everyone in the area. There are a few arm chairs, some placed between the couches, and others placed sporadically throughout the room.

On the wall by the door, I notice there is a coffee cart complete with an espresso machine and some cookies. My stomach grumbles at the thought. I forget peanut butter and jelly isn't meant to hold you over the long term. Luca takes notice and goes to making us both a coffee and grabbing a small plate with a few different sweets options on it. I take one more look around at the art on these walls. The colors are bright, startling in contrast to the modern décor of the lobby. I can tell this room is meant to be more inviting and warmer. The pictures are of flowers, beautiful landscapes, gardens, and it is all done so tastefully.

We walk over to a couch next to the arm chair that Darcy is now seated in, talking with Demora who is on her opposite side also in an arm chair. I take in the twenty or so other people in the room and realize that everyone looks so friendly and upbeat. I feel myself relaxing into the couch with Luca beside me, his hand resting on my knee holding the plate of cookies for me to choose from. I look around and see that everyone is also relaxing back into their seats and a sea of calm falls over us. Demora rises to her feet and I piece together that the vibe of this room is all thanks to her. I am constantly amazed by her grace and serenity.

"Welcome everyone! I am so pleased you were all able to attend this evening's meeting. I know we are missing a few and this isn't our normal meeting time but we have a new member I wanted to introduce you all to. But first, I would like to begin with us all going around the room and giving our name. Feel free to share as much or as little as you like but let us all remember, this is a safe place. Sasha, how about we start with you?" I hope there isn't a pop quiz about this later because I am already feeling anxious about remembering all of this. As soon as the anxiety starts to kick in, it is washed away and I look over to see Demora is smirking at me. I smile back and listen in to Sasha.

"As you already know, my name is Sasha. I am an executive assistant to the board members here at The Alliance. I am the one that has the shield protecting this place from the public's eye and keeping it secret from the SGP." I am envious of her strength but grateful for it because she has allowed this wonderful place to exist without fear of destruction. I make another mental note this evening to give her a second chance. A man stands up beside her and I can tell he totally takes full advantage of the gym on the property. He is tall and extremely broad with veins protruding from arms and hands. When he speaks, his voice is a deep boom.

"My name is Adam. My ability is super strength." Everyone around me then giggles and I see that Alex is also smirking. Did I miss something? "I'm kidding. People just take one look at me and assume that is all I am good for but I actually have a photographic memory. I can look at the page of a book, never actually read it, but I can then recite to you whatever was on that page from start to finish. It is really both a blessing and a curse. Great for when you need to pass a test but horrible for when you want to actually enjoy a book... or bear witness to something you wish you could forget." He takes his seat and around the room we go. I am amazed by some of the things that I hear, things that I only thought existed in books.

There is Janet who can put thoughts into your head as if they were your own. Tristan can speak and understand every language in the world, something he believes stems from being an old soul that has lived a lifetime in every culture. Christian is a tracker using smell, something he compares to that of a blood hound, and goes on to tell me about the time he tracked down a missing four-year-old girl who had wandered off and was gone for three days. Jessica can melt metal, Antwon communicates with the dead, and then we land on Carlos.

Carlos looks to be about fifteen years old with jet black hair, bronzed skin, and chocolate brown eyes. He has a gentle face but looks to be very tall. He still has the lanky boy build that young boys have when they enter high school and he is quiet but, when it is his turn, there is a mischievous glint to his eyes.

"My name is Carlos. I am originally from Phoenix, Arizona but I moved here when Darcy found me. My father was abusive and my mother worked two jobs so when they learned that I could read minds, they feared I was mental. My dad tried to beat it out of me and my mom cried in horror at the thought of having to check me into a mental institute. Thankfully, I found this place and want to assure you that I have it under control. No longer does my head get flooded with other people's words and I am able to only use it when I want to and with other people's permission." I think back to the thoughts that I had just earlier in the hallway and breathe a sigh of relief to know he hadn't heard them. "Although I must say, I don't have to be able to read minds to know that your hormone levels are elevated and that you are thinking of very adult things that include my friend Luca there... and I may have heard some of your thoughts before you entered the room and before I could turn off the waves you're sending off. You know, if you need a roo—"

"CARLOS! I appreciate you sharing your personal story but I would like to remind you that you aren't supposed to share the things you hear or see in people's minds either. It is an invasion of privacy." I have never wanted to escape from a room faster.

"Actually, I can smell the elevated hormone levels and would have to agree with Carlos for once," Christian adds. Now the entire room is in an uproar of laughter at my expense. I throw my hand over my face and try to peek at Luca but even he has his eyes squeezed shut with laughter. Darcy has her hand over her mouth and is trying to hide her giggles as well but Demora looks absolutely horrified, mirroring how I feel right at this moment. Suddenly the calm vibrations come over us like a tidal wave.

"Gemma, I believe you are our last member to go this evening. Are you ready?" I take in a deep breath and exhale slowly. Luca takes my hand in his and gives me a reassuring squeeze.

"My name is Gemma Jacobs. I have only known about my abilities for about a week now. I had a vision that came true. I have also dropped in on something that that was currently happening as I slept. I also have learned that I can project thoughts and things I imagine. Just this afternoon, Luca and I were in Jamaica... figuratively speaking of course." Another hand squeeze so I continue. "I am still figuring things out because it is all still a bit of a surprise to me. I hardly think that one vision come true really makes me psychic and I don't think that it is really that big of a—"

"Do you have any idea who your mother is?" a quiet girl whose name I can't remember pipes up from across the room. Perhaps it's Amy? "That is why you're getting special treatment and why we were all told to attend this. The glorious Genevieve's daughter has come home again." She gets up and leaves the room. The room is silent for a few moments as the door clicks closed.

"So, can you show us that projection trick you were talking about? I don't know about anyone else here but I sure could use an escape from reality." Christian is smiling at me and I can tell that it isn't malicious but is in fact friendly. I appreciate the subject change and I am taken aback by the comments Amy made. Are all these people really here because they were told they had to be on my account? What is her problem with me anyways?

"Yeah, I suppose I could give it a try. I haven't done it for this large of an audience before. I really have only done it with Luca and Demora."

"Oh, we know you've done IT with Luca." Carlos gives me a very exaggerated wink and before I can protest, he says, "I am only kidding! Gemma, if you're going to be hanging around here, you have to lighten up and live a little!" Everyone once again laughs and this time I too join in.

"Okay, any suggestions, Christian? Or anyone else have any ideas?" I look around the room but nobody does even so much as open their mouth.

"How about somewhere that is special to you? Maybe it'll tell us a little more about you." Demora's suggestion reminds me of the trip I took with Grace in the sixth-grade. I remember her telling me that this will always be our special place and while I am sitting here surrounded by people that will never know her, I need to find a way to feel close to her again. I need to feel like I haven't just replaced her with Luca and that her memory won't live on with me.

    I close my eyes and imagine the smell of the city streets. There is a pretzel and hotdog vendor standing to my right. You can barely hear yourself think over the sound of taxis whizzing by and cars honking left and right. My feet are shaking from the subway passing underground. There are big buildings everywhere. Models adorn the billboards in advertisements for Calvin Klein, Victoria's Secret, and some new perfume that can be found at Macy's. People are bustling and shoving past one another, not taking the time to say hello or wave. Everyone here is on a mission and niceties aren't necessary. I am standing in the middle of Times Square just like Grace and I did when we came with our families. The lights are bright as night settles in around us and it is just another warm July summer night.

    When I feel that I have the picture perfect in my mind, I open my eyes in awe. The people around me are now standing with their mouths agape looking up at the moving advertisements. The room that was once comfortably lit by lamps is exploding with the lights of Times Square. Though the people aren't bustling on the streets and we are the only people here, everything else is present. I look over and see that Janet is standing at the food cart with a pretzel in her hand. Christian is standing next to a manhole cover that has steam billowing up from it. Luca's face is turned toward me and I feel giddy with excitement over sharing this with all these people that were so open to me.

    Carlos is trying to hail a taxi as it flies by but isn't successful. It is all so real and I am watching the crosswalk lights change when Antwon appears beside me.

    "Gemma, this is all so amazing. Someone is here and would

like to join us but she said you have to let her in." Goosebumps cover my skin when I realize that Antwon, who can talk to the dead, must be referring to Grace. Closing my eyes, I picture her there with us too and as I picture the way her blonde hair falls around her shoulders, I feel a hand on my shoulder. I open my eyes and there she is, smiling, wearing her favorite hot pink mini skirt and a white tank top to match. I can't help but smile.

"I am glad that with all the fun you've been having in my absence that you still chose this as your special place," she says suggestively, her eyes flickering over to meet Luca's.

"Oh Grace, I wish you kne—" She puts her hand up and stops me midsentence.

"I do know. I know that you're still feeling guilty for living while I am gone but, please, honor me by living it to the fullest. Remember me by visiting the places that we loved to go, by doing the things that we loved to do, and by continuing to bloom into a version of yourself that I always knew was there hiding behind the surface. This is amazing, Gemma. And you..." she turns her eyes back to Luca "...take care of my best friend. Or I will haunt you and that is a promise."

"I promise. I promise on everything." Luca wraps his arm around my waist and I am so ecstatic that my best friend and my... whatever he is, got to meet even if it is under the most unrealistic circumstances. I feel Grace's arms around me and she whispers, "We will discuss your afternoon at a later date." And then, just like that, she is gone again.

"Thank you, Antwon." He smiles and walks over to join Janet at the food cart who is now helping herself to making a hotdog. I am curious as to if she can actually eat it or not but at this point, nothing would shock me. As we stand there, Darcy and Demora both tell me how amazing this is. Christian thanks me for taking him to New York for the first time. A small girl that I think is named Lola tells me it is just like she remembered it and I just marvel at the fact that last week I was ordinary and this week I feel extraordinary.

When Luca drops me off it is just after nine thirty and my dad's car isn't in the driveway. I assume he is out with Abigail but I am relieved that I won't have to face him tonight. Before I can get out of the car, Luca does a perimeter sweep and listens to see if we are alone before walking me to my door.
 "Thank you for everything today. You have been so great and I swear my life is not normally this messy." I turn to Luca, wrapping my arms around his waist.
 "Thank you for being messy and spending your whole day with me." He tucks loose hair behind my ear before leaning in and giving me a soft, sweet goodnight kiss. "Goodnight. I'll be listening for you." I open the door and watch his retreating back, feeling my heart sink at the thought of being away from him.
 Once I am ready for bed, I crawl under my covers and turn off the light. My dad still hasn't made it home but I am more than okay with that. I feel safe knowing Luca is close by and I fall asleep instantly.

I am in a dark room, the only light coming from a small lamp in the corner. There are people talking and I walk closer to the sound of their voices, careful to not make any noise or sudden movement. By the lamp sit Hughes and Adams. There is a figure standing with their back to me but looking at them. I can't make out what they look like but they are female and they begin to speak.
 "If you two can't figure out a way to get the girl here, I will

be forced to intervene. If I have to intervene, there is no need for you to work for me now is there?" Hughes and Adams both shake their heads and mutter a "no ma'am" before the woman continues, "This is getting ridiculous. What is standing in your way?"

"It is Luca, ma'am." The mention of his name makes the hair on the back of my neck stand up. He is getting dragged into this and I feel a sudden urge to protect him. "He never leaves her side." For once Adams seems that he is at a loss for words.

"Find a way. I don't care who he is or who is mother is. He will not stand in the way of what I want. Do I make myself clear?" Hughes and Adams nod. I try to get closer to get a good look at the woman but I stumble over a rug and bump into a table. Hughes is on his feet shielding the woman behind him and Adams moves closer.

"Who is there?" But before anyone could spot me, my eyes fly open and I am back in my bedroom.

I am sitting straight up and breathing ragged, fearful that they knew it was me in the room. Did they see me? I look around the room and find that I am alone. Now I am worried because Luca always comes running when these things happen and I will never forgive myself if something happens to him because of me. As I toss back the blankets, I feel the air from my ceiling fan hit me and chills spread through my body as the cool air hits the sweat I am drenched in. I quietly pad over to my window and, as I am about to open it, my heart leaps out of my chest when Luca surprises me on the other side. I am both relieved but also suffering from a minor heart attack as I unlatch the window and slide it open to allow him entry.

"You all right? I heard your heart rate increase and you were breathing heavy. You don't look so good either." Concern creeps across his face and I feel slightly insulted by his comment... until I spin around and see my reflection illuminated by the moon in my full-length mirror. The hair that isn't slicked to my face with sweat is standing in every other direction. I am pale with sunken eyes enveloped in dark circles and my clothes are damp from the night sweats.

"I thought you'd find this charming," I say deadpan and then remember that I am so happy to see him for a legitimate reason. "I had a drop in. It wasn't a vision of a future event but I think it was happening right now. When I was there, I bumped into this table and it moved, making a screeching noise in its wake. They heard it and they reacted."

"Who are they?"

"Hughes and Adams and some woman. I think that she is their leader."

Luca scratches his chin for a moment and then tells me, "That can't be. Their leader is Elijah."

"Are you positive? They've used that name in one of my visions. What can he do?"

"He used to be with The Alliance. He was in charge of acclimating the new people as they joined. But he got too power hungry and decided to join SGP. They moved him up through the ranks because they liked what he brought to the table... mind control." I can't believe the odds that we are up against.

"Maybe I should just turn myself over to them. I am what they want. That is all they keep saying and they said they'll stop at nothing and nobody can stop them. It is safer for everyone involved if I just quit fighting them." I try to take a step away from Luca but he catches my wrist, pulling it to his chest.

"Gemma, you listen to me. You are worth the risk. You are worth the fight. There are a lot more people on our side than you met just hours ago. They will help you. I will help you. Please don't give up." I feel so defeated. Here is this boy that I want to protect so desperately but he wants to protect me just as much. I turn away from him again but this time grabbing his hand and pulling him along with me. I climb into my bed and pull the blankets back, making room for him. He slides in laying on his side facing me. He pulls me into his chest and kisses my hair. With our arms wrapped around each other and my head buried in his chest, we fall asleep and I have a dreamless night.

I awake the next morning to an empty bed. I can hear my dad fumbling around downstairs in the kitchen so I am sure Luca escaped before he could be discovered. I am just slipping into my white Converse when there is a knock on my door. I open it to find my dad standing there awkwardly, shifting his weight from one foot to the other and back.

He is in a pink dress shirt and navy dress pants with a pink and blue striped tie. He offers me a cup of coffee that he has already prepared in my favorite mug, one that my mom used every day with a watermelon on it that says "you're one in a melon". It was a cheesy mug my dad picked up for her at a truck stop when we took a road trip when I was ten. She loved it so much and just the thought brings a smile to my face.

"Mind if I come in for a few?" I take the coffee from him and lead him into my room, mentally checking to make sure there isn't any trace of Luca left behind. I sit on the corner of my bed and my dad takes a seat across from me in the chair.

"I know yesterday was uncomfortable and I am sorry. I am sorry that I didn't tell you and that you had to find out that way. I was trying to find the perfect opportunity but then everything happened with Grace and I didn't want to bombard you with too much all at once." I take a sip of my coffee and ponder what he said, trying to formulate the perfect response because up until this point, I didn't even know how I felt about the situation. But knowing how happy Luca has made me over the last few days, I know that my dad is deserving of the same happiness.

"Honestly, Dad, it's okay. It has been three years of you being alone so I understand. I just want you to be happy but can you promise me something? No more secrets? I feel like that is all we have right now. Secrets about Abigail and Mom, the things I can do, tip toeing around each other's feelings... you are the only family I have and I want to be able to talk to you." Dad smiles and it crinkles his eyes in the corners. I meant what I said. I don't want secrets. I want open communication between us.

"Thank you, sweetie. When did you become so grown up and mature? I promise, no more secrets. But while we are discussing secrets, what is going on with you and that boy?"

Ugh this is not the conversation I wanted to be having with my dad. I try to change the subject but then my phone chimes. I reach for it and see a text from Luca. All it says is, "BOYFRIEND 😊 That is... if you'll have me?"

I am speechless but I turn to my dad and tell him, "I guess you could call him my boyfriend."

"Is he a nice boy? He seems like a gentleman." If only my dad knew that Luca was listening in on this full conversation.

"Dad! He is great. Very kind and just a genuinely good person."

"Great! Then you two won't have any problem with joining me and Abigail for dinner tomorrow evening. Cooking out here at the house. I want us to all get to know each other." Seeing my dad so happy makes it hard to hold a grudge and now that I am apparently in a relationship of my own, I have no issue with him moving on with his life. He has put me first for the last three years and I never stopped to think about him needing someone too. As he turns to go, he spins back around to face me and says, "He isn't a Red Sox fan is he? You know they aren't allowed in this house."

I laugh and shake my head. "I don't think so but I will be sure to double check before this goes any further." He smiles and then exits my room, shutting the door behind him.

My dad hangs around the house for most of the morning, working from his laptop at the table. Luca takes the opportunity to run home for a quick shower and visit with his mom for a few. He figures that the SGP don't normally like to include civilians in their affairs and they'll keep their distance from the house until my dad leaves. Around eleven thirty he decides to head out for an inspection on one of his listed properties and I decide that I will be driving my truck today. Where? I am not entirely sure but I do know that I can't hang around here all day and Luca will have to suffer through my driving for once.

As soon as my dad's car is out of view, there is a red Honda pulling into my driveway. I watch as he climbs out of the driver's seat, wearing black jeans, a white shirt with thin black stripes, and red vans on his feet. He is truly so beautiful that I can't believe he is actually interested in me. I was just always 'Grace's friend' when it came to boys or they wanted to race me at track practice, borrow my notes, cheat off my homework but never has anyone looked at me the way that he does.

I throw the front door open and leap into his arms, surprising the both of us by wrapping my legs around his waist and then planting little kisses all over his face while he laughs at me. Finally, my lips find his and I can't think about anything other than how soft his lips are and the way they move so in sync with mine. His mouth opens and I seize the chance to suck on his bottom lip a little and then let him explore my mouth. As we kiss, I can hear Mrs. Welsh in her backyard watering her plumerias three houses to the left. The Reynolds' family dachshund just chased a squirrel up the tree five houses to the right. I can smell honeysuckle blooming nearby and baby birds in the tree in the backyard are chirping for their lunch. We finally pull away and Luca puts me down.

"So your dad is gone... an empty house... and you're my girlfriend now soooooo?" The devilish grin on his face makes me want to lock the door and not let him out of the house but I need fresh air and don't want to run the risk of my dad returning earlier than anticipated.

"Don't go getting any ideas! I have decided to take you on a field trip for the day. As in I am driving us to a place of my choosing and we are taking Tonya."

"Tonya? Is that a friend we are picking up on our way?"

"No. Tonya is my truck. Tonya the Tacoma. So let me grab my keys and my bag so we can get out of here." He smiles at me like it is totally not a normal thing to name your cars but we've always done that in our family. Mom drove Maximus the Maxima, dad drove Brittany the Beemer for a while, and so I have Tonya the Tacoma.

We drive with the windows down and David Bowie again playing through the speakers. Everyone has always thought I was strange for liking older music but Bowie had a way with words that makes you want to shout them at the top of your lungs. Only this time, I opt for just singing along and decide the shouting will have to wait until I am alone. We figured with the SGP practically tracking me and showing up out of thin air that we might as well just live our lives to the fullest and deal with them as they come.

I decide to take Luca to the park where Grace and I used to come for playdates when we were kids. It has baseball fields, soccer fields, a sand pit for volleyball, basketball courts, a playground, and lots of green fields shaded by trimmed trees for families picnicking. We would play on the playground and then our moms would sit us down and we would all eat lunch together. It is a special place to me and it always seemed romantic as I watched couples strolling on the trails hand in hand. I also thought it would be a place that offers us a little privacy to talk.

We walk hand in hand, a blanket tucked under my arm that I keep in my truck for spontaneous moments like this, until we find a quiet space under a couple of trees across from all the chaos of the playground. Being a Friday, the place is pretty quiet aside from the moms and toddlers and a few joggers pass us by on the path that circles the entire perimeter of the park.

I lay out the blanket and we take a seat, me opting for sitting cross legged while Luca sits next to me with his legs stretched out, leaning back on his palms.

"How many other guys have you shared this blanket with?" I swat his arm playfully and turn to look at him. "You want to talk some more about the dream encounter you had last night or should we just pretend we came here to take in nature's beauty?"

"For your information, I keep this blanket in my truck because I like to come out here and read from time to time. I find it peaceful but to answer your question, I don't want to talk about it and I want to just enjoy a little time with my BOYFRIEND without having to talk about the fact that I am a circus freak." Now Luca playfully swats at me and breaks into the wide grin that relieves all the tension I carry in my chest.

"All right then. What do you want to talk about? This is your field trip so I'll allow you to call the shots."

"Hmm…" I tap my chin with my index finger as if I am deep in thought but I know exactly the things I want to ask him. For starters: "Why does Sasha already seem to have disdain for me? Did you guys date or something at some point?"

"You picked up on that? I was hoping you wouldn't." He rubs the back of his neck and I now know that it is a tall tale sign that he would rather discuss anything else, like the big bang theory would be better than this. "When her mom left a year ago, I tried to be there for her. I felt bad because she became a shadow of herself and she seemed so alone. I started spending time with her, taking her to do different things like the movies, miniature golf, bowling, so I guess I could see where she thought that there was something more but there really wasn't. As a matter of fact, all that stopped when I started spending my time with you… can I tell you something?" I am so intrigued that all I can do is nod my head yes. "The night that Grace died, a week ago today actually, we were at the same movie. Sasha and I were sitting in the back row and you and Grace were a few rows ahead of us. That was the first time I laid eyes on you and Sasha kept catching me staring at you but I couldn't help it. You had on that light blue shirt that hugged your body just right, white capri pants, and your white Converse. I should have known her intentions were different than mine when she elbowed me when I watched you get up and walk to the bathroom. Then after the movie, I walked her to her car and she tried to lean in and kiss me. I explained then that we weren't more than friends. I kind of disappeared from there because then I came to you that night and I haven't been able to leave your side since." He looks at me with such tenderness that I blush. I blush because he was looking at me before he even knew me. I blush because I am ashamed that he is so beautiful but he noticed me and I hadn't noticed him. I blush because he was attracted to me even before I needed protecting. I lean over and kiss his cheek, so grateful for his presence.

"It is no wonder the girl doesn't like me then. She thought she had you in her grasp and then I show up and ruin it all for her." I bring my palm to my face like I am truly sorry for stealing his heart but I will never apologize for what we share. "Okay, next question, lover boy. What was Amy's problem with me?"

"Ahh yes. Amy. Your mom brought Amy to The Alliance when she was only nine. Your mom helped her with her abilities before she left but, when your mom walked out, Amy suffered too. She was thirteen at the time and she had no family to return to. She is a little bitter about it still, as you can tell." I wish I hadn't asked because now I don't feel bad for Amy but I feel angry with her. How dare she treat me the way that she did because my mom left her. How does she think that I feel? I am her own daughter and to know she helped others but left me to fend for myself makes me sick to my stomach.

"I'd like to say I feel bad for her but I don't. She can join the club of people that my mother let down, me included. She may have lost her mentor but I lost my mom." I am frustrated now, drawing my knees up to my chest and wrapping my arms around them. I may look like a pouting little kid but I don't care.

"You're right. I am sure she is just jealous... because you somehow bagged The Alliance's most eligible bachelor." I look at Luca and he winks at me in a very over dramatic kind of way.

"Oh my god, shut up! You are so full of yourself!" I shove his shoulder but he grabs my arm and pulls me into him, causing us both to fall over with me landing on his chest, pinning him to the ground. We are both laughing so hard that we can hardly catch our breath. When we finally pull it together, I realize I haven't moved off of him yet and our eyes are locked on one another.

Luca lifts his hand, tucking hair behind my ear and running his thumb down my jaw line. As I lean forward, he is lifting his head up to meet me half way and we are kissing.

How I managed to go the last eighteen years without ever really kissing a boy is beyond me but now that I have, I am glad that it is Luca. He is practically a stranger to me but I also feel like I know every bit of him, like our souls are somehow connected. I can hear a little boy sliding down the slide all the way across the park as he comes to a screeching halt at the bottom. I can hear the mulch landing with a thud against the playground equipment as another little boy throws a tantrum because he doesn't want to leave the park yet. He screams, "Just five more minutes!" I can hear the runner breathing heavy on the opposite side of the trail and hear the rhythm of his shoes on the pavement. Every time we have a deep, passionate kiss, my senses are ignited like the world comes alive around us and leading up to this moment, everything was asleep and dull. Luca literally has breathed life into me.

He is the first to pull away and gazes up at me, licking his bottom lip. I never thought that I could get turned on just by little things like the way he tilts his head to the left when he is really looking at me. Or the way that after a kiss, his eyes blaze even more fiercely. Not to mention the way he sometimes sucks his bottom lip between his teeth making me want to just kiss them all over again.

I reach up and trace my finger over the scar above his eyebrow. It is about an inch long and almost blends into the color of his skin. If you didn't really look at him closely, you would miss that it is even there.

"How'd you get this scar?"

"Oh this?" he asks, reaching up and touching it. "I must've

gotten this when I fell for you. So about this dinner tomorrow night, are you up for it?" He changes the subject and I don't want to push it. Whatever it was, he will tell me when he is ready.

"Actually, I really think I am. I will take any excuse to introduce you as my boyfriend. I could really get used to saying that word. Luca Andrews, are you my boyfriend?" I ask flirtatiously, batting my eyelashes for good measure and taking on a southern drawl.

"Why, Gemma Jacobs," Luca replies with a very phony and thick southern accent, "I would be honored to be anything you need or want me to be. Especially your boyfriend." He gives me a soft kiss before we decide to readjust. He goes back to sitting with his legs extended and leaning back on his hands while I opt for laying down with my head in his lap. He is stroking my hair as I talk and I love looking up at him when he talks. The way the sun lights up his face, puts his high cheekbones and chiseled jaw on full display. I still can't believe that he is mine.

Chapter 10

Saturday night rolls around fast and I can't contain my nerves. I don't know if I am more anxious for Luca to get here or more worried about facing Abigail after the way I acted on Thursday. Dad is skipping around the house like he is from some 70s sitcom, singing to himself while he flips the steaks in the backyard. I was put in charge of making the salad and just watch him through the kitchen window. I really am happy that he is so happy. I haven't seen him act this way since... well since before my mom walked out.

I have the table set for four and I am just putting the finishing touches on the salad when the doorbell rings. I smooth down the front of the sundress I opted for and check my reflection in the microwave before scurrying down the hall to the front door. I swing it open not sure who I was expecting to be on the other side but surprised to find both Abigail and Luca standing on the doorstep. Nobody knows who should speak first but then Luca hands me a bouquet of flowers and I notice that Abigail is holding one almost identical to mine.

"I brought these for you." He steps forward and kisses my cheek. I blush before turning to Abigail.

"Hi. I just... I just wanted to apologize. About Thursday. It was just a surprise to me but I would really like if we could start over. Think we could do that and you forgive me for being a giant pathetic loser the other day?" Abigail laughs and I am again taken aback by how gorgeous she really is. Her blonde hair is hanging in loose waves halfway down her back. Her lips are just as red as the day I met her and her make up is absolutely perfect. She has a brilliant smile and legs for days that she shows off in her white cotton sundress. Apparently we were going for the same sort of look this evening.

"I would really like that, Gemma. Luca here was just going on and on about you. He sounds like someone else I know." She is peering over my shoulder and I turn to find my dad standing there, face aglow. I slide out of the way and invite them in.

Abigail walks toward my dad as Luca whispers in my ear, "Did the flowers say I am working too hard to win her approval and your dad's? Getting them for Abigail was my mom's idea." He throws his hands up like he is afraid I will be mad but I just shake my head no.

"It isn't too much. It is just perfect. Your mom raised you right. SUCH a gentleman." I take his hand and lead him toward the kitchen.

Dinner flies by. Everything about it is so easy and laidback that I can't believe I was stressing this whole time. Dad and Luca have really hit it off. They are discussing basketball and the decades old debate on if Michael Jordan really is the greatest player of all time. Every once in a while Abigail will pipe in and I realize there is more than looks that drew Dad in. She clearly has a love for sports like he does.

I learn that she is a personal accountant and just recently relocated here from Texas after a bitter divorce. Her ex-husband didn't want children, but she very much did, and it drove a wedge between them. She is eight years younger than my dad and she enjoys running too. We agree that we will make plans so I can show her the best places to run around here. She, like me, prefers to run out in the open and off from a treadmill.

"Honey, I haven't seen you run in a long time. You aren't spending too much of your time with Mr. GQ over here, are you?" I groan and feel like dying of embarrassment. Before I can answer though, I feel Luca give my knee a squeeze under the table.

"Actually, Mr. Jacobs, we were going to go running tomorrow. Gemma thinks that she can beat me so we have a bit of a bet going on here." My head snaps up to look at him. We do? I didn't even know we had plans to go running.

"Really? And what does this bet exactly entail?" my dad asks suspiciously. He is leaning forward, elbows on the table, looking directly at Luca. "Because I can tell you, my little girl will make you look bad and I am not sure your ego could handle that." We all start laughing and the seriousness disappears. I forget how great my dad's sense of humor has always been.

"Well whoever wins gets to pick what we do on our next date."

"That sounds like a great time!" Abigail pipes up and then narrows her eyes at me. "You better kick his ass!" I smile at her and think how nice it is to have a woman in the house again. She isn't my mom but I don't think she is going to try and be. I don't get that vibe from her. I just feel that she already fits in so well with us and I barely know her.

Luca tells me goodbye at the door after we clean up the kitchen together. Dad and Abigail retire to the backyard to drink wine and talk so I decide to give them their privacy. I tilt my head back waiting for his kiss but instead he brushes his lips against mine and whispers, "Meet you upstairs? Open the window for me? Because that sundress has me wanting to kiss you in ways that wouldn't be appropriate at your front door."

My body shudders in anticipation and I am already figuring

out how to excuse myself to my bedroom for the night. "Be there in five." I practically shut the door in his face and try to not appear too anxious as I walk out back and tell my dad goodnight and tell Abigail it was a pleasure to spend the evening with her. As soon as I turn the corner to the staircase and I am out of view, I am sprinting up the stairs and straight into my bathroom.

I brush my teeth and mid mouthwash, Luca is behind me wrapping his arms around my waist and pulling me flush against him. I am so thankful that my bathroom is connected to my bedroom. I rinse my mouth and spin around, pressing him against the wall.

"What is it with you and getting me into a bathroom?" I ask as I start kissing his neck. My heart is racing and I want to feel him pressing down on me. I want to feel his kiss and his touch. Another shiver courses through me and I grab his hand, dragging him over to my bed. When we reach the edge, I push him down so he is sitting and then climb on his lap.

This feeling of confidence and feeling sexy is a foreign concept but I haven't ever felt freer and more alive in my life. His mouth is on mine, hungry and possessive as I take his face in my hands. His hands are gripping my waist and pulling me against him. I start grinding my hips and hear him sigh against my mouth. I take that as a good sign and continue my torture upon him, holding nothing back. Our breathing is heavy and we are trying hard to keep the volume to a minimum, thankful that my dad doesn't have super senses. There is a thrill in making out with a boy and groping each other knowing we could be caught at any time.

Luca slides my dress up and grabs ahold of my butt, pulling me both in and down against him. I can't think straight. The only thing on my mind is taking things to the next level, a level I have never been to and always feared to go. I am yanking off his shirt and in the same movement, he slides my dress over my head. I take in his broad shoulders, the way the moonlight breaks through my window and shines on the muscles layering his back, the look of lust in his eyes and the swollen redness of his lips. Before I can talk myself out of it, I climb off his lap and start to undo his belt buckle, unfasten the button, and I am sliding off his jeans. I leave his boxers on just for the benefit of torturing him a bit longer. He is watching my every move as I push his knees apart and get down on mine in front of him. I look up at him through my eyelashes and see his chest is moving rapidly, heart racing, and he has no intentions of stopping wherever I decide this is going to go. Wherever I take it, he is along for the ride.

    I draw back his boxers and I see him for the first time. It takes my breath away and the feeling in my stomach knots again at the thought of him. Trying hard to maintain my confidence, I take him in my hand. The moan that escapes his lips presses me forward and gives me the reassurance I need as I stroke him slowly, I keep going. I am fueled by the way he wraps his hands in my hair, the way he pulls the hair back from my face, and the way he is looking at me when I dare to steal a peek through my lashes.

    He lets another moan out as I pick up the pace and I realize that I am enjoying all this power he has given to me in this moment. I am going to be what makes him come undone. I will be the reason he orgasms. He calls out my name, and I know I have him close as his hips lift from the bed. He grabs my face bringing my mouth to his.

    I take his lip between my teeth and I finally understand what he was saying about how its fulfilling just to know the other person is satisfied. I tighten my grip and start alternating between slow and fast speeds. He throws his head back and I hear him under his breath. "Fuck, Gemma. Oh my God." As he comes on my hand. I stand up and go to the restroom, washing my hands and reveling in how empowering this feels. Looking in the mirror, I can't miss my flushed cheeks and I feel so relieved to overcome this initial hurdle.

When I walk back into my room, he is laid back on my bed with his hands over his face, breathing is still ragged, and when he feels my weight on the bed next to him, crawling over toward him, he sits up and takes my face in his hands.

"How in the – where in the hell did you learn to do that?" I feel bashful now and can feel the blush tinting my cheeks.

"So it was good then?" I ask sheepishly, marveling at the way his face is flushed and feeling like I am seeing him in a whole new light.

"It wasn't good. It was fucking amazing. I have never – never has it ever felt that good. I can't wait to see what else you've been holding out from me." He takes my face in his hands and plants a wet kiss on my lips.

I lay down, pulling him with me. He has his forearms on either side of my head, hovering over me and kissing me slowly and passionately. He pulls back to look me in the eyes, brushing stray hair from my forehead, and I realize how perfectly content I am right now. Being in this moment with him and him looking at me like I hung the moon, makes me feel so very complete. He kisses me one last time before rolling over and taking me with him so I am perfectly positioned on his chest. My head rises and falls with every breath he takes, his hand rubbing up and down my back and the other resting under his head.

"Thank you," I say to him, mimicking the very words he said after he pleased me.

"Thank you?" he replies with a chuckle. "What are you possibly thanking me for?"

"For being the first person I have ever been intimate with. For not pressuring me or holding my inexperience against me. For making me feel comfortable and just for being... you I guess." Luca is quiet for a while in return and I feel self-conscious all of a sudden. Did I say something wrong? Was that coming on to strong? I start to lift my head but he pushes it back down.

"Gemma. I want to be your first everything and I find your 'inexperience' refreshing." I relax knowing I didn't overstep and close my eyes, letting his heart beat and the sound of air filling his lungs practically sing me to sleep. Right before I feel sleep take over, I hear him whisper in my hair, "I am falling so hard for you."

I wake up on Sunday to a bright stream of light through my window, bathing my room in a soft, warm glow. I can't help the smile that breaks out across my face as I recall the night that I had, the night we shared. I look to my left and find that I am sleeping alone but in his place is a note. "Gone to get running clothes. Will be back before you know it. Be ready for our afternoon run!" I had completely forgotten all about the run he spontaneously planned at dinner last night. I secretly wish he had forgotten too because, without even stepping outside, I can already tell that it is another hot North Carolina summer day.

I slide out of bed and tug on my running shorts, a white sports bra and tank top, then have to dig through my closet to even locate my running shoes. There was a time when I felt I lived in them, but it has been weeks since I have put them on. As soon as my feet are tucked in to the maroon and white Asics, I feel the muscles in my legs burning just begging to be used. One last step before heading downstairs, slicking my hair back into a high ponytail, and then I am ready to go.

As I descend the stairs, I am greeted with the mouthwatering smell of maple bacon sizzling in the kitchen. There is an aroma of freshly brewed coffee and I hear the toaster pop up. I come through the door to find Abigail in a pair of black yoga pants and a gray Johnny Cash t-shirt. I would have thought that the sight would have upset me, made me think about my mom and act out because another woman has so easily fallen into her place but instead it makes me smile. She seems so fun and bubbly as her hips sway and she is quietly singing Uptown Girl by Billy Joel, all while flipping the bacon. She turns to grab the toast from the toaster and spots me, scaring her and causing her to drop a slice of bread.

"Gemma! I am so sorry. I hope I didn't wake you. I... is this weird? Me being here this morning? If it upsets you, I totally understand!" Her face is alarmed, and I can tell she is worried. I honestly can't say that I blame her given the way that I treated her in Tiffany's the first time we met but I think that after last night, I proved to her and my dad (maybe even myself) that I am totally one hundred percent on board with their relationship. My dad's happiness means more to me than my own after he has put me first for so long.

"No, Abigail! This is perfect! I can't remember the last time the kitchen got this much use all at once! And it absolutely smells amazing." I smile and genuinely mean it. It is nice to have another woman in the house. "I love your shirt by the way. Are you a big Johnny Cash fan?" She looks down as if she forgot which shirt she opted for this morning and then looks back up at me smiling.

"Your dad did mention you have a stellar taste in music. To answer your question, yes, I actually grew up listening to him. I absolutely loved his voice. So full of sorrow and strength. My daddy grew up listening to him with his daddy so it was only fair they handed it down to me... and did you see pictures of him when he was young? Mmm mmm mmm." She winks at me as she starts to butter the toast. "Don't tell your dad I said that." She starts to laugh as he walks in the kitchen.

"Don't tell me what?" He is laughing as he walks over and drapes an arm around my shoulders. "What can't dear old Dad know?"

"Oh, just that Abigail burned the toast. I told you we needed that new toaster!" She and I share a knowing smile.

"This thing is so touchy. It is almost as ancient as those brown dress shoes you insist on wearing every day." We all laugh and I think again about how perfectly she meshes with us. It is almost like she has been here all along. This may be a good thing for Dad and me. "Gemma, you sticking around for breakfast?" Just then there is a knock on the door and I already know that on the other side, there is a boy that I am absolutely crazy about. I break into a run to get to the door, throwing it open and find Luca smiling back at me. His smile is like the sun rising after an endless train of gray days. I jump into his arms and hug him tight, like I didn't just sleep with him beside me all night, and then we hear my dad shouting from the kitchen.

"Luca, get in here and join us for breakfast!" Luca looks to me for a sign on how to respond so I subtly nod my head yes.

"I would love to, Mister Jacobs." He puts me down and crosses over the threshold making his way to the kitchen. When we walk through the doorway, Abigail is already setting the table for us. Bacon, toast, scrambled eggs, and fresh fruit are all set in the center with glasses of orange juice. My dad extends his hand to Luca, giving it a firm shake before adding, "Please. Mister Jacobs makes me feel too old. Call me Peter." And then, he leads Luca over to the table while peppering him with questions as to how was the rest of his night, did he have a long drive home? Luca looks to me and we share a knowing look before he gives my dad the answers he wants to hear rather than the truth. I hardly think my dad wants to hear that we fell asleep wrapped up in each other in the room right down the hall from where they slept.

As I take it all in, my dad here, Luca, and now Abigail, I feel like for the first time in a long time that everything is going better than okay. I feel light and happy and like the last three years were a necessary step to finding this. Now this, I wouldn't trade it for anything.

Chapter 11

We have been jogging on the trail around The Alliance for about ten minutes and I can finally feel the burn subsiding in my legs. After not using them for so long, I have to work through the pain so I can reach that runner's high. I used to think that it was a lie but now I am pushing myself trying to get there. Luca is doing a good job of keeping up with me, not once asking for us to take a break, but I can hear he is breathing a little heavier than me.

The trail is gorgeous, just like I thought it would be. Covered by large mossy trees so the heat isn't totally unbearable, the path winds through the trees and fields surrounding the property and I try to think of a more beautiful place to run but I can't come up with any. There are birds in the trees chirping along, a slight breeze is rustling the branches, and the sound of our feet beating against the dirt path is like music to my ears.

Before we started running, we stopped in the building and said hello to Darcy and Demora, grabbed a couple of bottles of water from the kitchen, and headed out. I led Luca through my stretches, most of which he laughed at, and then we took off. We haven't done much talking, mainly because it throws my breathing off, but also because the peace and quiet is comforting. I love that when we are together, we don't have to fill the time with unnecessary chit chat. We get to just enjoy each other's company and live in the moment.

We are rounding a corner that takes The Alliance out of sight when Luca stops, hands on his knees, and head down. I turn around and continue to jog in place, so my muscles don't get cold. It is hard to maintain the same momentum when you take breaks and have to warm your body up all over again.

"I'm sorry. Just need – a breather." He manages to pant out between deep breaths. I check my fitness tracker and see we've done 1.75 miles in twelve minutes. Not bad but also not my best. I can already feel the sweat trickling down my back and beading my forehead so I take a swig from my water bottle and look at Luca. He is red in the face and I feel horrible for putting him through this excruciating heat. We picked the hottest part of the day to run but I can't lie… it sure feels good.

"If you can go three quarters of a mile more, I will let you kiss me and seduce me." I smile at him in a way that I hope says come and get it, then turn and start back down the path. Not even a second later, I hear the sound of his feet pounding behind me and before I know it, he has passed me.

He is rapping Eminem, "You only get one shot so do not miss your chance…" and he is running faster than my dad when he hears that dress socks are buy two get the third free at Dillard's… man has a strange obsession with those dress socks.

I start to laugh but try to catch up without blowing my pace completely and when we finally hit the 2.5 mile mark I yell "Time!" Luca collapses on the ground sprawling out, face covered by the shady trees, and breathing like it's his last breath. "Oh come on! It wasn't that bad!" I protest while taking in his sweat drenched t-shirt and the way his hair is stuck to his face.

"Not that bad!" he manages to choke out between breaths. "I don't even have the energy to cash in on my seducing. Rain check?" I walk over and bend down, kissing his salty lips before smirking at him.

"As if you even needed to run the race to be given the chance to seduce me." He reaches out and grabs my wrist tugging me down on top of him.

"Now that is a very unfair way to play it, Gemma." But I can tell he finds it funny and now our sweaty, sticky bodies are touching. Usually when I sweat, I run for the nearest shower and avoid contact with anyone. Even a high five after a race grosses me out but there is something so sexy about being sweaty and touching him. I can imagine the sweat coming from another activity, and that is a total turn on. Suddenly a thought crosses my mind and I have to ask.

"Did you run with me today because you actually wanted to or is this an attempt to protect me while allowing me to do something I enjoy?" He looks over at me thoughtfully for a second before looking back up to the sky.

"Honestly? It is a little bit of both. I know The Alliance is supposed to be the safest place for you so I shouldn't have to worry. I have also left you alone a few times when I felt it was safe. You know, running home to change this morning and shower the other day, but other than that I haven't been away from you. However, I also wanted to run with you because I don't like being away from you." He looks back to me and his eyes bore into mine, melting my insides to where it feels like lava is coursing through me.

"I don't like being away from you either. I feel an emptiness now when you aren't around." Surprised by my own honesty, I look away. Being vulnerable has always been hard for me but not with him. He makes me want to just spill everything, all the innerworkings of my mind, the darkest secrets in my soul. I want him to know everything and anything.

"Do you believe in soul mates?" he asks me, peering at me quizzically, like the answer to this question means everything.

"Honestly?" I ask, using his own words against him. "I don't. I just feel like… if there is such a thing as soul mates does that mean that my dad will never love Abigail the way that he loved my mom? Or do people not get a second chance at love, and if they do, does that mean that they haven't found their soul mate at all? What happens if a husband or wife dies and then they move on eventually? Is that to say we only get one love in our lifetime if things don't work out as planned?" Luca's brows crease and the corners of his mouth turn down a little bit. He looks away but I feel his hand come to rest on my hip.

"Yeah, I suppose you're right. Kind of stupid huh? Forget I even asked." His voice trails off and then I realize the conversation is over. I can't help but wonder if it was something I said? Did he expect another answer? I know most girls are hopeless romantics, soul mates, *Romeo and Juliet*… the whole sordid tale but I am not entirely convinced. Then again, I haven't ever been in love, this is the closest I have ever been, so I don't think I can really have an opinion on the matter one way or the other. At least, I don't think I have been in love. Am I now? It has to be too soon right?

While I am trying to sort this out in my mind, Luca shifts away from me and stands, reaching his hand down to help me up. I stand and dust off the back of my shorts before taking his hand and starting the walk back to The Alliance. I can see the stone structure in front of me, standing tall and resilient in the middle of nowhere. I could get used to the tranquility here and how calm it seems to be. Almost like it exists all on its own, no outside world can infiltrate its walls. No outside chaos can disrupt the sanctity of this place and I hope the same goes for mine and Luca's relationship.

When we make it back inside, entering in through the massive front doors, I see that Sasha is back. She wasn't here when we came in earlier, out running an errand I believe is what Demora said. Now here she stands with her red pencil skirt, black blouse tucked in, and black heels. Her long dark hair is in beach waves and her eye makeup makes her light freckles more noticeable. I see the way she looks at Luca with a glimmer in her eyes before she looks over to me and smiles. I can tell it is forced but after hearing about their history, I can't say that I wouldn't feel the same way. Gorgeous boy goes from spending time with me to dating another girl practically overnight? I would definitely feel the same.

"Hi, Luca!" she says a little louder than necessary and almost as if she realizes this, she says softer, "Good to see you again, Gemma."

I don't have to force the smile I return and tell her, "Yeah, you too." I lean into Luca as we start to make our way to the kitchen before she calls us back.

"Oh wait! Gemma! I forgot. This was at the gate for you." She hands me a tiffany blue box that is tied with an ivory bow. The box is about the size of a box that jewelry generally comes in. I look to Luca who looks back at me, just as confused as I am and I can tell we are both sharing the same thought. Who is this from? Just then Darcy walks around the corner.

"Did you kids enjoy your run?" She is all joy and sunshine until she spots the befuddled expressions on our face. "What is it?"

"This was at the gate for Gemma. Did you send her something?" Luca's voice has gone up an octave and his eyes are pleading for his mom to say it was her. That there is nothing we need to be worried about here. Darcy instead looks over to Sasha.

"Sasha, where was this? How did you find this?" Darcy is trying to maintain her calm demeanor.

"It was just sitting outside the gate. Security said they didn't see who put it there but that their cameras glitched not too long ago and immediately came back online. I don't know. Is something wrong?" Darcy places a hand on her shoulder.

"No, dear. Everything is fine. Thank you. You can go back to your desk now." Sasha turns and walks away and Darcy fixes her eyes on us. "I am going to go get Demora. You two head to my office. Don't open that box until we are both present with you. And do me a favor, don't stop and talk to anyone. I will see you there in a few." With a quickness in her step, blonde hair flying behind her, Darcy leaves up the stairs and disappears. Luca is now practically dragging me down a hallway that my tour didn't cover and I have to run to keep up with him.

I can feel my heart racing. Who left this? What is it? Why do Luca and Darcy seem so on edge? Luca finally stops at a door on the left that is shut and locked. There is a keypad on the door so I turn away to give him privacy as he taps in a few digits and throws open the door. When we enter, I see the office is almost the size of the library. There is a large dark wood desk, a few matching bookshelves sit behind the desk against the wall. There are a few brown leather armchairs, this room an extension of the neutral décor throughout the bottom floor. I notice on the desk there is a picture of Darcy and Luca on a beach with him standing behind her, their backs to the water. His arms are thrown over her shoulders and I can see that the smiles on their faces are almost identical. Something so beautiful about the relationship they share that it can even be captured in pictures.

"Here. Take a seat and try to breathe. I can hear your heart racing so just relax, okay? My mom and Demora will know what to do. They always know." Luca puts a hand on my shoulder and guides me to a chair, pushing me to sit, before taking the seat next to me. His hand comes to rest on my knee and we eye the box in my hands with suspicion. It is so quiet, I can hear the gentle whir of the air conditioner flowing through the room. The lights create a soft and comforting glow so I try to focus on the picture on the desk to calm my nerves. Luca catches me looking.

"That was taken back home in Cocoa Beach. It was the summer after my freshman year and my mom took the day off to spend with me. We went to Ron Jon's where she bought me a new board and wet suit. Then we went to this great taco dive that all the local surfers like to frequent after a day on the water. That day though, I didn't surf. We walked the beach and talked and she told me about her plans to move us here. This picture was taken right after she told me the news." Luca looks wistful, a small smile creeping across his face as the memory replays.

"Weren't you afraid to leave your dad and all your friends back home?"

"I was but I was more relieved. I was relieved because I thought I would be safer from the SGP. We were going to get away from my dad who always made us feel like we were freaks. We were getting a fresh start with people who were more like us. That was exciting for me after being surrounded by people that I couldn't share my experiences with." He looks to me now, head cocked to the side, and I reach my free hand over to stroke his cheek before trailing my hand up to his scar.

"What did the SGP do to you?" His mouth opens to answer my question as the door to the office flies open and in walk both Demora and Darcy. Instantly, I can feel that the tension and stress that I was feeling upon arriving in here has subsided and I know that it is the work of Demora. I nod to her a sign of thanks and she nods back, understanding what I am trying to nonverbally communicate.

"Gemma. Do you feel comfortable opening the package or

would you like one of us to?" Darcy pulls a chair so she's sitting practically in front of me as Demora walks around to stand beside her.

"I think I can manage." Shakily, I untie the ribbon on top and let it fall in my lap. The box has no markings to indicate where it could be from. Just a plain tiffany blue box with the lid taped shut on two of the sides. Reminds me of Christmas mornings when my mom would buy me clothes and I couldn't get into the box fast enough. I look up to the faces surrounding me, gulping down the nerves before I continue. I slide my finger under the tape on one side, freeing the lid. I take a deep breath before I flip the lid over, exposing its contents.

Inside the box is a sheet of ivory tissue paper fluffed to perfection and in the center, it is cradling a little pink flash drive. There is no note to indicate who sent this and I am instantly on edge, despite the attempt Demora may make at calming me, I can't begin to imagine what could be on this flash drive but judging by the sharp intake of breaths around me, the other three people in this room are wondering the same thing.

"You don't think—" Luca starts before Darcy interjects.

"It is impossible. We are shielded. How would they know?" She walks around to her computer, typing in her password, her face illuminating as the screen comes to life. "Gemma, would you mind bringing that over here? We need to find out what it contains." I stand and slowly walk over to stand across from her and hand her the flash drive before looking to Luca. His face is as white as new fallen snow and I can feel my palms start to sweat as the worry and anticipation builds. The flash drive loads and a folder appears with my name as the title: "GEMMA JACOBS". Darcy looks to me for permission to continue but all I can muster is a head nod.

Luca is standing behind me now, arms around my waist in a protective manner and eyes peering over my shoulder. The file contains photos. Darcy clicks them open and there, before all our eyes, is my last week. They are in no particular order. There is a picture taken of me and Luca kissing on the blanket at the park, a photo of us slow dancing in Tiffany's, a picture of us laying by the lake with him reading Twilight and I am munching on chips. The pictures continue to us sitting down for dinner with my dad and Abigail, Luca is cutting up his steak and we both wear easy smiles. Those easy smiles feel like a lifetime ago though they were just yesterday. There is a picture of us asleep in my bed, the moon light glowing through the window, my back pressed against Luca's chest and his arm tight around my waist. These are all such private and intimate moments, and I am so glad that they stop there and don't contain any more incriminating photos.

The very last slide is a video of us eating breakfast just this morning. There is a voice over but you can tell they used a voice disguiser. It sends chills down my spine as it talks over the easy banter we shared throughout breakfast. "Gemma. Do you really love these people? These people that you call family, friends, your own boyfriend? Doesn't their safety mean anything to you? We've tried this the nice way, Gemma. Now we aren't going to be as understanding. You join us or slowly, the people you love and care for, will be removed from the equation. Consider this your final warning. You have twenty-four hours to reply." Then the video shifted to a logo with SGP in bold red letters. I turned burying my head into Luca's chest and feeling the cry catch in my throat. Tears streaming down, I feel him start to rub small circles on my back, his chin resting on the top of my head.

Feeling embarrassed from all this attention, I turn to Darcy and Demora. They look back like I just might be a ticking time bomb set to detonate at any second. "I need to just go to them. Maybe I can work something out. Maybe if they realize how my abilities aren't that special and I really am not worth all of this, they'll back off?"

"My child. Do you have any idea what you are capable of? You keep selling yourself short. You haven't honed in on all your skills but, trust me, you are a force to be reckoned with and they know that. Tell her, Darcy," Demora urges her on.

"Demora is right. Do you know how I found you so quickly? You lit up my radar like the fourth of July. The only other person to ever burn as bright as you is Sasha's mom. You have so much stored inside you that you haven't even scraped the surface of everything. Besides your visions, dropping in on moments in your sleep, and projecting your feelings, you seem to possess some way to talk to the dead too. I know you've been able to communicate and even conjure up Grace and touch her! Do you know how major that is? You can't go to them. You have to let us protect you."

"I'll be safe here, right? This is the safest place for me to be?" I am hoping for the reassurance. Scanning around the room at the three faces looking back to me, I don't think that I am going to get it. I feel a panic attack coming on. Taking a seat, I begin to rock back and forth and try to control my breathing. It is not an easy task because the way everyone is acting tells me I have every reason to believe that this is not good.

"The concern here, my love, is that if the package was indeed dropped at the front gate, then they know we are here. Either someone has sold us out or the shield isn't as effective as it once was." Demora seems truly puzzled but I lose sight of her face as the room starts to spin and blackness envelops me. The last thing I can make out is Luca calling my name and his arms sliding under me as my body collapses to the floor.

Chapter 12

When I awake, I am laying in what appears to be an old hospital bed, the seafoam green walls are familiar, and I am trying to remember where I am and why. Just then, Sasha peeks her head in the door looking genuinely concerned.

"Oh thank heavens you are awake. You gave us all a scare! I told Darcy I would look after you and let her know when you awoke."

"Wait. Sasha, where am I?" She spins and looks at me as if I have lost my mind and I am starting to think that she may be right. There is one other white metal bedframe in the room and a TV mounted on the wall but it still isn't making any sense to me. When I visited the old hospital, it had been transformed into something modern and homey. This? This was exactly as I had seen in my visions.

"You're on the second floor of The Alliance where we keep the living quarters for our residents. However, we didn't get a chance to redo all the rooms yet. Sorry, all the more up to date ones were taken but I know this is only temporary." She gives me a sympathetic smile and leaves the room, giving me a chance to take a look around before more company joins me. I look over to find a nightstand with a lamp and a small alarm clock. There is a bathroom in the front left corner of the room but all I can see from where I sit is the shower curtain and the sink. I realize that I am freezing and start to shiver. I look in the closet across from the bathroom to see if there is a blanket in there, but I instead see my maroon track duffle bag on the floor. I grab it and cautiously make my way to the bed, setting it down and peering inside. The bag is thrown together haphazardly, and I can see there are a few different outfits, my toothbrush, toothpaste, and a hairbrush. I look over to the nightstand again and realize I overlooked my phone plugged into the wall. Next to my phone is Grace's urn. Whoever took the time to prepare this bag obviously knows that this is something I would never leave behind.

I am beginning to panic all over again when Darcy enters the room and takes a seat beside me. She puts her arm around my shoulders and begins to run her hand up and down my arm in an attempt to create friction and warm me up. The room lights up from the lighting coming through the window at the back of the room and I can hear the rain hammering down. I am trying to place all the pieces together. Something about seeing this duffle bag, being in this room, Darcy sitting this close, something about it unsettles me and I can't put my finger on it until Darcy speaks.

"Don't worry. You're safe here and your dad is safe too. Everything will be all right. He and Abigail are going to stay right down the hall." Thank goodness he is so close. But I suddenly realize that I feel very empty and alone. I feel like part of me is missing and, as crazy as that sounds, that is how I know that Luca isn't here on the property right now. Somehow, I am able to detect when he isn't close.

"Thank you so much, Darcy. Where did Luca go?" I fidget with my hands and look at her face, warm and smiling, doing her best to make me feel comfortable and at ease.

"He just ran back to our home to pack a quick bag. I think we are all going to stay here until this passes over or we figure out a solution. I don't want you to stress it though! The Alliance is used to handling these types of situations so hang tight and it'll get resolved. Let us handle it!" She rests her cheek against the top of my head. In the short time I have known Darcy, a very short time indeed, I have felt nothing but loved and cared for. Almost like our time together has been years and not merely days. Her love reminds me of the love Mrs. Jennings always gave me. I feel warmer but my stomach still feels dread and I can't remember why. That is, I couldn't remember until Demora rounds the corner. Before the words can even leave her mouth, I feel my body break out into a cold sweat and tears prick the corners of my eyes.

"Darcy! It's Luca." She is as stiff as a board, and I can tell it is taking everything she has to be standing upright. "They've got him." The sound that escapes Darcy is not one I will ever forget. It was somewhere between a scream and a sob as she fell into my shoulder and started crying. Demora makes her way over and grabs her, spinning her around until they are making eye contact.

"Listen. I know you didn't want to tell her this but I think she needs to know. She must know so we can help Luca." Darcy is using her eyes to plead with her, desperation written all over her face.

"But he isn't here! He should be here when she finds out. It isn't fair to them! I don't want to rob them of this moment. He begged me to wait until the time was right! This isn't the right time!" Her face is growing redder and wetter the more she cries. I realize they must be talking about me. I am the only one in here. Who else could 'she' possibly be?

"Darcy, darling, I understand. I truly do. But if we don't tell her, there may never be a time for us to tell her. We may never see Luca again. They may never be given the opportunity to live it out. We must do it!" Demora's eyes are just as sad as Darcy's and I can feel the tension radiating through this room. Darcy is missing her son. I am missing my boyfriend. Demora is trying her best to keep us afloat but the words still haven't sunk in. This all seems like a bad dream, like the horrible visions in my head but that's exactly what this is. A vision that I dreamt and that is now coming true. I feel so weak.

There is a rap on the door and we all turn to find my dad standing there, his black sweatpants and gray Yankees shirt signaling that he was dragged out after he had prepared for bed. What time is it anyway?

"I just wanted to check on you, peanut. Make sure there isn't anything I can be doing? I hope what I brought you was enough. You know, these ladies are very demanding when they need to be." He smiles warmly at them both before reading the mood of the room. "Is everything all right?" He went from calm to on the edge in a matter of seconds.

"No, Dad. It isn't okay. They've got Luca and I need to get him back." My dad crosses the room and throws his arms around me. Finally I can find the tears that have been threatening to fall ever since I put two and two together to realize where this vision was taking me. I sob but then I feel selfish because I have only had Luca a little over a week. Darcy has had Luca for nineteen years. I have no right to be crying and she has every right to fall apart. I release my dad from the death grip that I have on him and dry my eyes. I look at these two brave women that have become pillars of strength in my life. "What do you need to tell me?"

"Okay fine. Meet us in my office. Five minutes. The code is 0211. Luca's birthdate." Darcy turns toward the door and makes her exit with Demora holding on to her the whole way. They are whispering but I can't make out what they're saying. I try to compose myself the best I can.

"Dad, are you going to be okay here? Until this is all over? I am so sorry that you're in this situation. It is all my fault." I look down at my shoes and the sting of the truth hurts. This is all my fault. If I hadn't had those visions. If I hadn't fallen for Luca and gotten pulled into this life. If I hadn't just agreed to be a part of the SGP instead of resisting them... everyone would be safe right now.

"Don't you worry about me, Gemma. You do what you have to do to bring that boy home. You protect yourself. I have Abigail and we have already met quite a few interesting people in this place. I think we are going to be just fine. That goes for you too. Everything will be okay." He hugs me again and I inhale his aftershave, the same one he has used since I was little. I feel the softness of his t-shirt fabric and I reminisce on the time that he went to a convention out of town, and I slept in this very shirt for the three nights he was away. Mom practically had to pry me out of it. I pull back and look at his face.

"In case I haven't told you lately, thank you for being such a great dad." He smiles as I reach for my hoody that is in my bag and I head out the door to Darcy's office. I feel like I am on a top-secret mission. Mission bring home the boy. Mission rescue Luca. Mission kick some SGP ass for messing with the people I care about. I take the stairs two at a time and find Sasha at the front desk, tears trailing down her face and her bottom lip quivering. I assume she heard the news.

"I am so sorry, Gemma," she squeaks out as I approach her desk.

"Don't be sorry, Sasha! You didn't do anything. This isn't your fault. We will find him." I try to sound convincing, but I am still shaking from getting the news myself and I am trying to tell myself that I need to be strong for Darcy's sake.

"It is my fault," her voice drops to a whisper, "I am the one that delivered the package." She looks down at her hands and I remember something. Sasha is the one in charge of the shield. She is the one that is supposed to protect this place and keep it off the SGP's radar but she failed. And she is the one that delivered the package.

However, now isn't the time to point fingers and it certainly isn't my place to lay into her over it. Instead, I just give her a small shrug and make my way down the hallway to Darcy's office. I can hear hushed voices on the other side but I can't make out what it is they're saying so I put the code in and enter.

Darcy and Demora are sitting across from one another, Demora's hands on Darcy's knees trying to soothe her but I am sure even her abilities reach a limitation and can't conquer all the feelings Darcy has coursing through her right now. Upon my entry, they both look up and gesture for me to sit in the chair to the left of Darcy. I take my seat but I can feel adrenaline rushing through my veins and I am afraid of whatever it is they've been keeping from me. Demora opens her mouth to start but Darcy cuts her off.

"Gemma, have you ever heard of 'destinati amantes'?" I shake my head no. That doesn't even sound like we are speaking the same language here. "It means destined lovers in Latin. We have this belief in our culture, our culture being those with abilities, that we are born with a destinatum amarotem, but we don't always find them." I'm not understanding where this is going.

"You mean, like soulmates?" I ask hesitantly, my mind reeling back to the conversation that Luca and I had just this afternoon. Was that really just hours ago?

"Uhh kind of… but it is much more than that. When you find your destinatum amarotem, you're drawn together like magnets.

Your souls just click, you perfectly align, and complete the other. Your abilities become more powerful together and if the connection is really strong, you can even share abilities between the two of you. Does any of this ring a bell?" I nod my head yes.

"When Luca and I kiss, really kiss – oh gosh this so embarrassing." I bury my head in my hands but Darcy urges me on, Demora on the edge of her seat hanging on my every word. "When we really kiss with passion, I can experience things at a much higher sensitivity than normal. I begin to hear things that I hadn't heard before even from a great distance. I am hyper aware of my surroundings." Darcy's hand flies to her mouth and I give her a second to calm down. She fans her face and takes a deep, gasping breath.

"Honey, we moved here because your mom told us we should. But there was more to it. Luca felt a draw to this place, and I was never able to figure out why until the day that I met you. When he insisted on protecting you, I was surprised. He avoids the SGP like the plague but when you were put at risk, a complete stranger to him, he stepped up and didn't leave your side. Then he told me about your kiss down by the creek and how he had never felt more alive and I knew it was more than simple first time puppy love. Then Reggie, you haven't met him yet, he came to me and said that he saw a future of Luca with a girl that matched your description and he said he saw that the two souls were completed with one another. Are you following?"

"Does Luca know what you're insinuating here? Is that why he asked me this afternoon if I believed in soulmates?" I feel the tears welling up again. I shot him down and he was trying to tell me something important. How could I have done that to him? I feel numb. From my fingers to my toes.

Darcy nods her head yes. "He wanted to find the right time

to tell you himself and he wanted it to be special. Do you feel this way? All those things? Do you feel them for my son?" I am in such a state of shock that I just sit there and stare at the two of them. I am thinking about these last nine days with Luca. I think about the way our hearts beat perfectly in sync, the way that when we kiss the entire world comes alive around us. I think about the emptiness I feel in his absence, and I think back to our first meeting and realize that I had felt something even then. There was a magnetism to him and, at first, I blamed it on him being mysterious to me in so many ways. Next, I blamed it on the fact that he was being so protective over me, but now? Now I can only blame it on the fact that we are destined lovers, destinati amantes, whatever you want to call it. As if a light bulb has turned on, I turn to Darcy and take her hands in mine.

"I feel all those things and so much more for your son. He is everything to me and it explains the fact that after such a short period of time, I love him. I love him and I need to be able to tell him that. So how can I help?" Her eyes fill with tears again but this time there is a smile on her face. Not her usual smile that lights up the room. This smile barely reaches her eyes but there is a certain relief behind it.

"I am so glad that after the time we spent here, him always feeling like something was missing and me assuming it was his dad, I am so glad that he found you. Remember the magnetism that I mentioned before?" I nod my head yes but still unsure where this is heading. "With your ability to drop in and your draw to one another, I believe you may be able to locate him. We will be with you and help you every step of the way. You've dropped in on us before and I know you've dropped in on the SGP before."

"Yes but none of that was expected. I didn't mean to do any of that. It just... happened." I have no other explanation for it than it just happened.

"My dear, nothing in this supernatural world of ours is a coincidence. Your subconscious brought you to that night where Luca and Darcy were talking because, unbeknownst to you, your souls were already attached. And as far as the SGP is concerned, I believe that was out of self-preservation because I can't think of any other draw that could possibly explain it. Meet me in the arena where we held circle in twenty minutes." Demora excused herself and left Darcy and I sitting alone.

"Darcy, can I ask you something?" Her eyes shift to mine and she gives me a small nod. "This destinati amantes, does it happen often?"

"Oh heavens no. As a matter of fact, I was beginning to think it was an old wives' tale because the only person I ever heard of meeting theirs was Demora and her husband died before I could meet him. But seeing Luca with you, it renewed my faith in it. I knew there was not another explanation for the connection you two have." Darcy pats my knee, stands, and then begins to pace. I decided to stretch and meditate to try and clear my head. Whatever Demora was going to ask of me wasn't going to be a light task and I wanted to give it my all if it meant bringing Luca home. He had to come home so I could look into his beautiful, icy blue eyes and tell him that I loved him.

When I enter the room, I see that Demora isn't alone. She has Christian with her. Darcy follows me in and shuts the door, locking it behind her. Not sure what the need for all the secrecy is but perhaps it is so we aren't interrupted and I can focus on everything. Darcy and I sit on the couch, opposite of the two armchairs that Demora and Christian occupy. I smell a candle burning in the corner of the room. It smells of gardenias, my favorite and I am instantly at ease and feel centered.

The storm still rages on outside but, despite the thunder and lightning, the fireplace offers us a comforting glow. The room is so quiet that I can hear the sound of the logs popping and crackling from the heat. We all sit silent, willing someone else to begin. Though I am not entirely sure why Christian has joined us, unless he is going to sniff for a trail, he is the one that starts us off. Taking in a deep breath and releasing it slowly, he begins.

"When we pulled up to Luca's house, sorry, your home Darcy, there wasn't a trace of anyone else around. Luca listened and peered in before entering but he said that nothing was amiss, so I waited on the front porch while he went to grab a few things. Everything seemed fine and I kept watch. However, after a few minutes, I started to smell panic and fear. The scent hadn't been there before, so I went running inside but he wasn't there. I searched everywhere and called out to him in the woods but no response and I couldn't catch his scent anywhere." Christian takes a pause but we are all on the edge of our seats. I can hear that he is getting choked up, his emotions are like a rollercoaster. I can tell by the way his facial features are set firm and unforgiving that he blames himself for what happened. I look at him intensely until his eyes shift to meet mine.

"Christian, this isn't your fault. Don't beat yourself up, okay? I am – we are – going to find him. I won't rest until he is here with us where he belongs." Christian nods and gives me a tight smile before continuing.

"So anyway, I went into his room and there were signs of a struggle. There were clothes tossed on the bed, his backpack was strewn and dumped out, his lamp had been kicked over but there was nothing. Not a trace, not a clue, nothing." Demora reaches over and pats him on the leg. Christian reaches for her hand and she gives it a squeeze before looking to me.

"Gemma, here is what I need for you to do. I can sense that you're already calm, centered. That is perfect. Job well done. Now close your eyes." I do as she says and focus on breathing. "Try to imagine a tether, a rope that ties you and Luca together. Imagine the tether to be thick and strong, unbreakable. Do you have it?" I nod my head yes. The rope disappears into darkness though, no idea where it is leading me but I have a feeling that it will lead me exactly where it is I am trying to go, to Luca. "Now follow that rope, follow it to wherever it leads you, never losing sight of it." I am marching forth, hands gliding around the rope as I pull it in more and more. There is a feeling of resistance as I tug like something heavy is on the other side. I am visualizing Luca on the other end. Picturing this rope tied around his waist and every step I take is bringing me that much closer to the boy that I love. I can hear the sound of voices in the distance but they are muffled so I try to move faster so I can get a look of where they are but suddenly my concentration is broken and my eyes fly open in response to the loud bang of a door being thrown open.

I startle, half expecting to see Hughes and Adams standing before me, but instead it is Sasha with a stunned expression on her face. As if realizing that she interrupted us, she begins to stutter out an apology.

"I am s— I am so so – I'm sorry. I came in to freshen up and I know this lock can be tricky so I thought it was just stuck and I fetched my keys and – oh gosh, I am so embarrassed." All of us just look at her, puzzled. Something seems so off about her since that package arrived. My thoughts drift back to our encounter prior to my meeting in Darcy's office.

"It is quite all right, dear." Demora reassures her, exchanging a look that doesn't go unnoticed with Darcy. "We were just finishing up for now. I think we all need a break and to get some rest because we have a long day ahead of us tomorrow." Everyone stands and I am sent straight into a panic. I can't take a break. There is no resting. I can't relax until he is back here with me. He isn't here to hold me when I have nightmares. He isn't here to call me princess or tease me or be overly protective like I am made of glass. I need him. I need to see his smile and feel his kiss.

"We can't break now! I was so close! I could feel it! Please! Darcy? Shouldn't we—"

"No, I believe Demora is correct. We need some rest. YOU need some rest. Especially after your fainting spell this afternoon. It is late." She shares a look with me that tells me not to push the topic any further. I feel there is something someone isn't telling me and it makes me feel unhinged. If we are all in this together, we need to be transparent and forthcoming with one another. "Trust me, Gemma. I want to bring my son home just as bad as you do but I know we are of no use to him unless we are rested." And with that, they all leave the room, passing Sasha at the door as they go. She looks to me with a fear in her eyes that I don't quite understand. Is she afraid for Luca or is there more than meets the eye with her? I stand to leave and follow everyone else out.

"You should get some sleep too. You look like you need it," I say to her as I pass and there is a new emotion that flashes across her face but I still can't get a good reading on her. Where is Carlos when you need him?

I climb the stairs two at a time and start heading to my room. I pass the room my dad is in and find that the door is shut but there is still light shining through the bottom. I can hear a TV on inside, sounds like some sort of sports channel. I really wonder how he feels about having to be wrapped up in all this and having to stay away from home in a place he didn't even know existed. I wonder if Abigail thinks I am a freak now? She just met me and is already being pulled into the fiasco that is my life.

I decide to knock and wait for a response. My dad answers and pulls the door wide gesturing for me to come in. I follow him inside and see they have one of the upgraded rooms. There is a queen size bed with fluffy white bedding like you'd see in a hotel. The bathroom is modern and there is a flat screen tv mounted on the wall. To the left of the door is a walk in closet and I can see a few outfits hanging in there. The dresser has my dad's watch, his laptop, and a purse on it. Abigail is sitting on the bed wearing her hair in a messy bun, no make-up on, and a Prince shirt on. If this were a normal situation, I would definitely strike up a conversation about her choice in 80s attire but normal is not the case here.

I sit in the arm chair to the right of the bed and Abigail mutes the TV, offering me a smile as she does so. My dad takes a seat on the edge of the bed and looks at me. I am stumbling to find the right words to say but luckily I don't have to because she speaks first.

"Listen, Gemma. I know you don't know me very well. I just want to say that if you need anything, I am here." I look up at her and see she is sincere.

"Dad must not have told you about me then… don't you hate me for all this?" I ask gesturing around the room. "You barely know me and you are totally uprooted and brought to this… place and you still offer to be my crying shoulder?"

"Gem, Abigail ha—" Abigail quiets him and places her hand on his arm.

"What your dad was going to say is that I actually have experience with this sort of stuff. My sister, Erin, has abilities. She can shapeshift objects, not people, but turning things like a fork into a violin. I've seen it happen." She chuckles as if she is replaying the memory and I am dumbfounded. Are these abilities more common than I originally thought? "So I have encountered the SGP before. I have heard of The Alliance and when I shared this with your dad, he told me about you. He thought that maybe since I had been on the outskirts of it with Erin that I could help you when you needed it." My face is warm and I have a knot in my throat. I am trying to hold back the tears and swallowing past the boulder that has landed on my chest is hard, my emotions are threatening to spill at any second.

"So you don't think I am a freak? You guys aren't mad at me?" I stare at the two of them.

"Absolutely not. You kidding me? I got a get off work free card! I can punch numbers anywhere... perks of being a personal accountant." She again smiles at me and I am again grateful for my dad finding her. I will have to personally thank him for that later.

"So, what happened to your sister? Oh God. You don't have to answer that. I am sure it is extremely personal." Abigail just laughs and tells me it's okay.

"She actually joined SGP despite us trying to convince her otherwise. She slowly drifted apart from us and then quit taking our phone calls and we haven't heard from her in about seven years. It is rough but that is all the more reason that I am going to help you fight whatever this battle is that you've got. I don't want to see what happened to Erin happen to you too."

"What about Luca?" My dad finally chiming in. My heart swells that he seems to care so much about Luca and his safety.

"I am going to find him. He is my... destined lover." My dad's eyebrows shoot up in alarm. "Don't worry. I am sure that Darcy would be happy to explain more about that later. But, if I have any hopes of helping them bring him home then I better get some sleep."

"Yes, young lady. I want to hear more on this later. Do you want to sleep in our room? I think that chair reclines. I saw your room is nothing compared to this suite." I can't help but smile at him.

"I think I will be just fine but thank you for the offer. You guys have a great night and... thanks for being here." My dad kisses my forehead and I surprisingly get a hug from Abigail before I walk out and quietly shut the door behind me.

I make it to my room and collapse onto the white sheets and stare at the ceiling. As if I could even sleep if I wanted to. I check my phone and see that it is 11.23. This may be the longest day of my life. Maybe with only the exception of the day Grace died only nine days ago. Feels like it has been forever. As I lay there thinking about her and thinking about Luca, I hear a gentle knock on my door. I look over and see Antwon standing in the doorway.

I sit up and dread instantly washes over me. "Please don't tell me you're here because—" Before I can even finish he is crossing the room and cutting me off.

"Oh my God, no. It isn't Luca. I'm sorry. I didn't think that by me coming by that would be the first thought to your mind! Mind if I sit?" He gestures to the bed beside me and I give him a nod yes. I don't know Antwon well. I know that he communicated with Grace for me so he will always be good in my book. Out of the corner of my eye, I take in his appearance. He looks to be about early twenties with close shaved dark hair, light eyes, and a smooth as silk dark complexion. It seems that everyone with abilities is remarkably beautiful and I can't help but notice how his eyes are almost the color of caramel. Feeling guilty for even looking, I stare back down at my shoes.

"I just came by because I know you're struggling right now. I know that you are having a hard time with Luca's absence, and I called out to Grace. She came and wanted me to tell you something. I believe her exact words were 'once a Jedi, always a Jedi'. Not sure if that has any meaning to you?" He looks at me quizzically without realizing that he just said everything I needed to hear right now.

"That means more to me than anything right now. Thank you for reaching out to her. She always knows what to say. Can you let her know that she can communicate with me every once in a while too?" Antwon's eyes go wide at the revelation.

"I'll let her know but, Gemma, I just want you to know… it is hard to move on and have closure when you keep looking into the past. Loss is hard enough without having to see the person and knowing they are dead." He stands and puts a hand on my shoulder before turning to the door.

I feel a tear slide down my cheek as he takes his exit and I lay back down staring back up at the ceiling. Grace knows that I love my *Star Wars*. She remembers the years of Jedis and Princesses. She knows that I always felt that the Jedis had the utmost honor and respect. That in a time of need and a time of battle, they were who I would have wanted to go to war with. And right now, this is war. It is a war on me and the ones I love. I close my eyes knowing that she has rejuvenated me and I have an idea. These visions always come to me in my sleep so maybe, just maybe, that is exactly what I need to do right now. Get some sleep.

It dawns on me suddenly that Darcy and Demora both know that I usually have these when I am sleeping. That is why they were so insistent that I get some rest! It makes sense now and I settle in and close my eyes, willing my mind to please shut the hell up so I can get some sleep.

As I drift off, I think about everything Darcy said. All the stuff about us being destined lovers and our souls being intertwined and I feel butterflies in my chest even through the pain because now I know, he was always meant to be mine.

I am in the same exam room as my dreams before. I am standing there in the corner and in comes the cloaked figure followed by Hughes and Adams. Between the two men is Luca with a sack over his head and his hands tied behind his back. Thinking back to the vision I had before, I now know who it is they are bringing in, whereas before it was a total surprise to me. They are practically dragging him to the chair in the center of the room. They've bound his feet to the legs of the chair, his wrists to the armrests, and once they removed the sack, they secured his head to the back of the chair. The large light above them shone directly down on him.

I try to take in as many details as I can. He doesn't appear to be hurt but there is a little cut on his lip. My guess is when they snuck up to grab him, he fought back. My heart is pounding in my chest at the thought of any harm coming to him on my account. I can't stand the thought of him in pain. He is angry with bloodshot eyes and the muscles in his arms are straining against the restraints.

"Tell us, Luca. Where is the girl that you've been guarding? Where did you put her?" the cloaked figure speaks, the same female voice that has been haunting me.

"She has a name. Her name is Gemma. You know that! I refuse to tell you. You aren't going to touch a hair on her head. Do you understand me?" Luca practically spits at her. It is taking everything I have not to rush forward and take his face in my hands but I know that information is wisdom and, right now, I need all the wisdom and details I can gather.

"My dear boy, do you think that her allegiance would lie with you if she knew the truth? Do not be ignorant. You are putting your life on the line for someone who wouldn't even choose you. So why don't you wise up and tell me where Gemma is." The cloaked figure laughs maniacally and chills run up my spine. There is something so sinister about her. She makes Hughes and Adams look like teddy bears in comparison to the evil rolling off of her in waves.

"You don't even deserve to speak her name after all you've done! And you better believe that I will tell her the truth because she deserves to know. But I will not give her up no matter what you do to me!" The cloaked figure takes a few steps back and signals with her hand to Hughes to walk forward. But before Hughes can unleash the fury that that I saw once before, Luca cries out, "Wait!" Everyone goes still and looks to him.

"There is something you should know before you assume that this plan of yours will work. Gemma and I, we are destinati amantes. You know what that means don't you? Yes I can see the panic in your eyes. It means that she will always pick me. Our souls are linked, we are intertwined, we are bound to one another." Luca has a devilish grin on his face and I know he is enjoying this. "You will always lose no matter what you do or who you are."

Just then, without any warning, Hughes stretches out his hands, a palm held out on either side of Luca's head and Luca writhes in pain. His screams make my blood curdle and I have to bite my lip from crying out. He goes still and the cloaked figure returns to stand in front of him. I still can't see her face or make out any of her features but her voice is icy as she tells him, "You think you can outsmart me? You must not realize that we are one step ahead of you. We already know where she is. We already know that she saw this very vision happening." Luca lifts his head to look at her and then I see his eyes land on me before quickly looking back to her, as if realizing he made the mistake of looking my way. "Ahh yes, Luca. We know she is even in this room right. This. Second." The cloaked figure spins around with her arms outstretched.

"Gemma I know you are in here. I know you are watching us right now. I have been keeping a VERY close eye on you. I am sure you were rather pleased with our photography skills. On the back of the property, you'll find a two-storey brick building, much like the one you sit in right now. The Alliance refuses to use this building due to all the... horrors that took place in it. Come here and come alone. We will know if you bring backup. It is time you came home."

My eyes snap open and my breathing is ragged. I look to my phone and see that it is 2.39 a.m. I know what I must do and I need to do it quietly. I slide my phone in my pocket and switch my Converse for my running shoes. I pull my hair into a high ponytail and carefully make my way down the stairs, trying my best not to make a sound. I decide slipping out the back door would be the best bet, afraid the front door will wake someone.

I tiptoe down the hallway but come to a stop in front of the picture with my mom. I look at how happy the four of them were, only two of them remaining. I wish that she were here to help me face this. I turn and continue my way down the hallway, easing the backdoor open, and slipping out into the night. The rain is still coming down and my shoes squish in the wet yard. I pull my hoodie up over my head, locking my eyes on a building in the distance, and I start to run.

Chapter 13

I slowly push the side door open but it does nothing to mask the loud squeak of the hinges. I cringe knowing that I just announced my arrival to the entire building. Though I have only seen Hughes, Adams, and the cloaked woman, I don't know who else to expect. I close my eyes and try the exercise that Demora was having me do earlier with the tether. Sure enough, the rope appears. I am walking, eyes closed, trusting that these instincts will lead the way. I am too afraid that I will open my eyes and lose sight like I did earlier but, suddenly, there is a door where the rope ends and I know that I have reached my destination.

    I glance around but there isn't a single soul in sight. The hallways are quiet, dark, and eerie. All I can think about is getting Luca and getting out of here. I haven't come up with a plan for after our escape… honestly, I barely even have a plan to escape. I should've thought this out a little better before coming but I knew that any more hesitation on my part would result in more pain on his. I take a deep breath and push open a steel door. It is heavy and groans as I apply more pressure and shove against it but I finally get it open and enter.

    My eyes have to adjust to the bright light that is in the center of the room, the same room from my visions. Surrounded by cabinets, the seafoam green color causing my stomach to churn, and in the dead center of the room sits Luca. His head is hung in defeat and my heart breaks when I see the sadness written all over his face. I cross the room in a matter of seconds, brushing his hair back from his face, and see his eyes are closed. The room is spinning and my blood turns to ice.

"Luca. Luca please. Luca please look at me! Please. You have to open your eyes. Luca! My love, my destinatum amarotem, please. I need you." I press my forehead to his and will him to open his eyes. Tears streaming down my face, I press my lips to his. They don't return my kiss and fear wells up in my chest. "I just found you. I can't lose you. Luca, please." I try a kiss again and this time, I feel slight pressure pressing back against me. My eyes fly open and Luca is looking back, his eyes still bloodshot and tired, but trained on me.

"You know? You know about us?" Despite the circumstances, I can't help but smile at him. His voice is soft and hard to hear but he is speaking. He heard everything I said.

"I do now. That is how I found you. Now we need to get out of here. I'm going to untie you." I first start with his ankles but with the knots so tight and complex, I am struggling to free him.

"You shouldn't have come. I can handle these people. You have to go! We don't have time to waste." He protests as I try to untangle him, finally getting one foot free. "Gemma, look, you have to go. I know who the cloaked figure you've been seeing is. I don't want you to go through facing her!"

"I won't leave you. I will never leave you, you understand me? Just keep quiet." I get his other foot untied, and I am about to start on his wrists when I hear a slow clap coming from behind me. I stand and slowly turn, shielding Luca behind me. In the shadows stands a large outline and I can already tell that it is Adams.

He walks into the light where I can see him, dressed in a black dress shirt and black dress pants. Shiny black shoes adorn his feet. He looks like he belongs at a formal get together and not in this ancient surgical room. I am surprised to find that he is alone.

"Gemma. Long time no see. Sorry we had to take your boyfriend to get your attention. No hard feelings I hope." A slow smile spreads across his face as he begins to walk circles around us. "I have told you that our leader does not have patience for dealing with the whole cat and mouse game. We were truly hoping you would come to your senses, and it wouldn't come to this. But you were rather persistent on avoiding us."

"Why should I join you? I know what you do. I know what you're capable of. I want to be no part of your program." He begins to shake his head at me, slowly as if I am a child that just broke a rule. What rule did I break and what are the consequences going to be?

"I think you'll change your mind when I show you what we have to offer you." He stops and faces me, now standing to the left of Luca's chair. "You are scared. I can sense it. You are worried. Worried about your father and about Luca. You are angry. Angry that we've caused so much rift in your life but what would you say if I told you I can make your family whole again?" He looks at me, his gaze never wavering, hands like a steeple in front of his chest.

"Don't listen to him, Gemma! It is a trick!" Luca is struggling against the restraints but I can't focus on him. Hughes now enters the room and stands across from Luca with only me separating the two. I switch my focus to him with my body still angled at Adams.

"Don't you touch him! Don't use your mental nerve shit on him either! Your 'leader' wants me so bad right? Hurt him again and I walk." I can feel the anger radiating off me in waves, my body temperature rising. I turn my eyes back on Hughes. "And you? What the hell are you talking about?"

"She said you would be feisty. She was right." He chuckles to himself. "But please. Don't let me do all the talking. Maybe we should just bring her in here to tell you herself." Adams gestures toward the open door and in walks the cloaked figure.

The face is hidden, it is like she is gliding on air as she makes her way toward me. I reach behind me and take Luca's hand in mine to let him know that I am here. I am going to get us out of this. I am trying to think of a plan as this unknown person gets closer and closer. She is only standing inches from me, almost at eye level, as her hands reach to the top of her cloak. I am holding my breath, afraid for what I will be face to face with once the cloak has been dropped. Remembering the evil dripping from her voice, the hair on the back of my neck stands straight up.

"She is afraid of you," Adams speaks up from my right side. It is hard to keep an eye on all three of them and make sure that nobody breaks through me to get to Luca.

"She has no reason to fear me," the figure speaks and the familiarity of the voice still hasn't registered. I just know that I have met this person at some point. Finally, the cloak falls and I feel the wind has been knocked out of me. "After all, I am her mother."

I stumble backwards, practically falling into Luca, as the words, cries, questions, and screams all get stuck in my throat. I am gasping for air and it feels like I am in a vacuum. There is no air left in this room and I am trying my best to stay on my feet. I can't pass out again. I can't afford to go down right now when I have no idea what is going on. My mother?

Before me stands the woman that braided my hair. The woman that my dad danced and sang with in the kitchen. The woman that kissed my bumps and bruises and promised that it would make them all better. Here is the woman that left me on my first day of high school with nothing but a note and a hole in my heart. That hole has finally been filled, patched, and repaired without any of her kisses. She wasn't there the day that I lost Grace. She wasn't there the day that I got my driver's license. She wasn't there the day I turned eighteen but here she is now and she is responsible for all the chaos in my life. I always hoped this day would come but now that it has, I am angry.

I am angry because she didn't show up when I needed her. She showed up when she needed me. She took the boy that I love, she chased my father into hiding, she has put us through hell and back by walking out and she made it even more hellish by showing back up. I take her in. She looks almost the same but with a harder edge to her. She doesn't look like the mom that baked cookies every year for the fall bake sale. Her auburn hair is longer again, tied back into a tight and serious ponytail. Her green eyes look wild and careless. The set of her mouth doesn't match the mother that read me bedtime stories but instead matches that of a hardened woman that rules with an iron fist.

"Is that how you treat your mother after all these years? Gemma, I thought we were closer than that." Her eyes almost look sincere but I can't fall for that.

"I thought we were closer too, Mother. Until you walked out on me and abandoned me." She rolls her eyes at me as if my words were too dramatic for her, as if what I said wasn't the truth.

"Abandoned you? Dear child, do you not realize that I was out preparing all of this so I could give you a better life when you came into your abilities?" She gestures around the room, but I know she is referring to SGP. Not The Alliance that she helped to build.

"Is this what your note referred to? The note that you left on my bed the day you left, is this what I would understand one day?" I can't keep the bitterness out of my voice.

"You remembered! This is exactly what I meant. I always knew you were a smart girl, Gemma. I didn't realize it would take you so much convincing though to join us so I really thought that we would be reunited under better circumstances." She looks at me almost apologetically. I look at her now and I feel like maybe I don't know her at all.

Suddenly, I have a strange thought enter my head. A thought that I feel wasn't entirely my own. The thought tells me to stall, draw out our conversation, help is on the way and I just need to hold tight and be patient. I piece it all together and know that Janet just sent that thought through to me. They know I am missing, they know where to find me, and they are on their way. I just have to wait and keep everyone's attention locked on me.

"You're right. Mother. I mean… Mom. You are right. But if you had come for me yourself, I probably would have come with you right away. I wouldn't have wanted to waste any more time." She looks to Adams who gives her a small nod. He is reading my emotions to check for sincerity, so I really must sell it.

"That isn't how things work, Gemma. There is a chain of command here. I am second in line behind Elijah. These two work for me." She gestures toward Hughes and Adams, both of them walking over to stand behind her, seemingly thinking that I will be cooperative now. "I can't just leave and go recruiting. But I sent my personal assistants to find you. Not everyone gets such preferential treatment." She smiles at me as if this news should make me fall to her feet and worship her.

"I have another question: if you helped start The Alliance, why did you betray them and go to SGP? You were already the leader there so why make the switch?" This question nags at me.

She sighs and looks to the ceiling as if the answer will be written there for her. She pauses before looking back at me, seemingly annoyed with my cold shoulder and questions.

"The power wasn't enough. There I had to run every decision by Darcy, Demora, and Margo. There wasn't enough freedom. We all shared responsibility and those people are just weak." She makes a face of disgust like we are talking about insects rather than the people that considered her to be such a great friend. "All they want to do is use their abilities for good. What a waste!"

"You know, Mom, I hear that our abilities are pretty similar. I've been told that mine are stronger, better if you will. At least that is what Darcy and Demora have told me," I say to her as a challenge. If I can get her consumed with something else, she won't notice when the others show up. I hear Luca behind me trying to get my attention, but I can't afford that right now. I have her right where I want her.

Mom snickers, the sound evil and menacing, and I can tell by the look in her eyes that she knows I am challenging her. She won't back down. I know she has always had a slight competitive edge but I was never on the receiving end of that. Luckily, it plays in my favor now.

"I am sure they did tell you that. They'll tell you anything that you want to hear. Those kiss-asses. And then to find that my daughter has fallen into their circle and gotten cozy with Darcy's son… repulsive." She sneers at Luca and I can hear his breathing intensify behind me. He is trying so hard to keep his cool. I wonder if Janet has put the plan of rescue in his mind and that is why he isn't trying to be more pushy or he just trusts me to handle this situation with my mother. Either way, I am grateful for his silence so I can process all of this.

"Well, I guess there is only one way to prove it, isn't there?" A slow smile spreading across my face, an idea pops into my head. "Why don't you go first and show me how it's done?" She closes her eyes and I prepare myself for whatever it is she is about to pull. I am extremely surprised to find that it isn't anything horrific or unfamiliar. Instead, we are standing in the kitchen of my home, the place she used to call home.

The pale yellow paint on the walls, the white cabinets with the white counter tops, and the stainless steel appliances are all exactly the way I remember them. Being here makes me homesick like I have been gone longer than a day. The magnets on the fridge hold up my school pictures, post cards from distant family members, and even the random drawing or two that Dad didn't have the heart to take down. Hughes and Adams are standing with their backs to the kitchen sink and sunlight streams over their shoulders from the window. Gone are the medicinal cabinets, the big light, and all the equipment. Luca is still, however, bound to the same chair. Mom is now standing in her apron, the pink and white plaid one, just like I remember it. I reach over to touch the French toast sitting on the counter, but my hand goes through it. I remember Demora's words now from the lake the first day that I met her. My mom's abilities are like holograms. They are there but you can't touch them. You can't smell them, and you can't even hear them. They are just... there.

A thought is suddenly pushed into my mind. It feels intrusive and not of my own but I listen to it anyways. The Alliance, a team of them, are heading quietly down the hallways now. I don't know how they haven't been detected but I know I must create a diversion and give them a sign when we are ready to pounce. Janet pushes an image into my mind now to let me know what the sign is. The image is of me extending my hand out to meet my mother's. Now the hard part is figuring out how to do that and make it look natural.

"Don't you remember all the mornings here, Gemma?" Mom's voice breaks me from my game plan and interrupts my communication with Janet. "All the cakes we made in here, all the family meals, all the times that you and Grace sat at that very kitchen table making sundaes with sprinkles and hot fudge? Sorry to hear about her by the way. The unfortunate price that had to be paid for me to know you had reached your potential." She's sorry? The price that had to be paid? She talks about Grace like she was a stranger instead of a girl that was like another daughter to her. She has no idea what my full potential is but I can already tell that, with her ego, she doesn't think my potential will ever reach hers.

"If you think so low of my abilities, that I am not going to be any better than I am right now, why the big chase and all the fuss? Why go to these extremes to try and get me to join your side if you'll always be better than me?" She seems taken aback by my comments, almost as if she is afraid because I am on to her. Hands on my hips, I await her response, fully aware that The Alliance is close by and waiting for me.

"Don't be silly. I don't want you to partner with The Alliance because you ARE better than they are. You are also my daughter and who better to introduce you to this world than your own flesh and blood?" I'm not buying it. But rather than argue, I need to divert her attention elsewhere.

"So be it. Let me show you what I can do now. Why don't we take a little trip to... say... the lake?" She rolls her eyes as if this isn't quite up to her standards, the selection of a true amateur. Little does she know, the lake has trees and water and uneven terrain. Perfect for trying to make a fast getaway when you understand the area and your opponents aren't as familiar with the surroundings. Luca and I know this shore and the walk through the trees like the back of our hands. Though I have only been out there a handful of times, every step I have ever taken with Luca is permanently ingrained in my brain.

I close my eyes and picture mine and Luca's spot. The water is touching the shore and rolling back in little waves from the passing boats. The sun is shining bright and beautiful, not a single cloud in the sky. The trees stand tall, the hills have their roots running through them at all angles like veins thirsting for life. There are birds chirping overhead as they glide through the sky together and you can smell the mist coming off the lake. It is peaceful and serene, a complete contrast to the mayhem that I know is about to unfold. I place the water to their backs and the trees leading from us to the exit, providing coverage and obstacles for when they pursue.

I look to them and see their mouths hanging open. Apparently, they didn't do their homework and didn't realize I was capable of doing what my mom can but that, in this case, I am better. I can make you feel it and smell it. You can reach out and touch it but, Mom? It is all an illusion. Kind of like my whole life with her was an illusion, an image of a woman that acted like every child's dream and turned out to be a nightmare.

She bends down, turning her back to me and places her fingers in the water. I watch as she retracts her hand and water drips down her long, slender fingertips. I look to Hughes, his head tilted back as the sun bakes his face, the rays dancing off of his skin. Adams is peering out over the water, taking in the surroundings across the shore.

My mom spins around and faces me. Her eyes are wide with wonder, and I think for the first time in her life she is left speechless. She touches her hand to her face and then looks up to the sun, squinting under its brilliance. I take a small step back and closer to Luca while they are distracted. Mom turns then and fixes her eyes on me.

"You are far more advanced than I gave you credit for." She clasps her hands in front of her as Hughes and Adams turn their attention back on me as well. "You would be stupid to let that power go to waste and I would like to think that I raised a smart child. Surely your father couldn't have undone my fourteen years of hard work since I left. I was, after all, raising you with a great purpose. It is time to embrace your destiny." It makes me nauseous to hear her refer to my father like he is merely a man that she passed on the street and not the person she met in college and spent twenty years with. "Join us, Gemma. Join me and I will help you hone in on your abilities and together, we can rule SGP and take our place where we were meant to… at the top over the weak who lack any abilities at all." She smiles as if she thinks my decision is that easy and for, argument's sake, right now, it is.

"Fine. But under one condition." I look back at her daring her to go against my wishes. She doesn't and, instead, she nods for me to continue. "Luca comes with me." He begins to protest as she scoffs, but I look at him and will him to just shut the hell up and work with me here. GO WITH IT. I turn my gaze back to her. "He is destined to be in my life and you seem like a person all about destinies, Mother. 'Taking our place at the top' would insinuate that you agree. So Luca comes or I don't go." She rolls her eyes as if I am just a puppy-love-crazed teenager and throws her hands up.

"I never pegged you as a girl that would need a boy. Or a girl that would let her entire future hinge on whether a boy could be her sidekick or not. Because, let's face it, child, he will never be on your level. But if that is what it takes to have you on our team, then I suppose we can pay that small price. I am sure that we could find SOME use for him. I know he was once heavily sought after by SGP but that was before me... I wouldn't have wasted so much time on him. He isn't worth that scar above his eye." So the scar is from them? I am angered but I can't let on that I am raging inside. I can tell she is trying to rattle me and cause me to backtrack, but it won't happen, and I know that now is my time to act.

"You know, Mom, you are absolutely right. We should just let him go and he can go back to those... peasants." I start untying his wrists. Adams and Hughes take an urgent step toward me but I don't stop. "I should have known better than to even ask seeing as how you turned your back on twenty years... I think I will be just fine erasing the last ten days." I look into Luca's eyes and see a sadness there but I try to give him a reassuring squeeze as I move to his head, releasing it from the back of the chair. "I also have to say, I am really glad that it was you that came back to get me."

"Is that so? Did you miss me?" I can hear her voice dripping in sarcasm and she can't hide the smirk threatening to take over her face. It is like she wants me to beg for her love and attention. Anytime I thought this scenario through, this scenario being seeing her again, I always thought it would be her begging for forgiveness. Knowing that Luca is now freed makes this next step an easy one.

"Of course I missed you. You are my mother, after all." I stand with one hand behind my back signaling Luca to stay put. "But it's more than that." I take a few steps closer to her, taking a deep breath because here goes nothing. With a sickening feeling, I extend my hand out to her and she looks from it back up to my face. It is like I am extending something poisonous her way or I am carrying the black plague. Finally, her hand starts to lift to meet mine and as soon as they touch, I look deep into her eyes that mirror my own and tell her, "I am glad it is you so I can look you in the face when I tell you that you are a selfish bitch and there is no way I will ever join your cause."

Shock spreads across her face as I clench her hand in mine and now I finally get to have the evil sneer. I change up the imagery a bit, moving in dark rain clouds as Hughes and Adams go to make a move toward me but the rain pelts them hard. There is a burst of people from the door and I feel Luca's hands on my shoulders.

"Gemma! Come on! We have to move!" I let go of her hand but she tries to pull me back, slipping in the process. We make a run for the door, through the trees standing between us and the exit. I glance over my shoulder and see the three of them are now in pursuit, slipping on the wet bank.

When I spin back around I am face to face with Sasha. Behind her is Janet, Demora, and a few others that I can't place their names or abilities. Sasha urges us to move. "Go! I've got a shield intact. Go! There are cars waiting out front to take us away from here." Sasha looks as scared as I feel so I do as she says and I run. I can feel that I am losing the lake scene as I climb through the trees, not understanding why it seems like we will never reach the door to this room. Knowing that Sasha has us protected now, I drop the projections and find that we have made it through the door and we are standing in the hallway. There are seven of us in total and the other three are close on our heels. I could tell that Hughes was trying to use his powers but they were bouncing off of the shield as we break into a sprint.

"I can't hold this forever! We've got to get out of here!"

Sasha runs at the back of the pack. I can hear the exasperated yelling of the SGP behind us.

My mother's voice is shrill in my ears. "Do NOT let them out of this building!" Out of the corner of my eye, I see Demora. Her face looks like a mixture of shock and sadness. I then remember that she was good friends with my mom and I am sure the monster behind us isn't the woman she once knew either.

We turn down a dark hallway and the doors to the outside are before us. I have Luca's hand in mine and I take a mental count to make sure we haven't lost anyone. Everyone is here as we burst through the doors and there in the driveway are two cars. I recognize Darcy's sleek Audi right away and behind hers is my dad's white Volvo. I lunge for the door, pulling Luca along with me and notice that Sasha is following closely behind me. The others pile into Darcy's car while Sasha takes the front seat and I shove Luca into the backseat before I climb in. As soon as our doors are shut, I see Darcy floor it and my dad follows suit.

Before we can pull away though, the door to the building flies open and my mom is standing on the sidewalk. I look to my dad's face and it is like he saw a ghost. His mouth drops open, face going white, and they lock eyes through the windshield. The darkness and the rain can't stop them from staring the other down, my dad in shock and my mom wearing a scornful glare.

"Was that—" but before he can finish, I cut him off.

"Yes, Dad. That is Mom. And let me tell you now. She is not the woman we once knew." I can hear my voice is tinged with sadness as we pull away and it doesn't go unnoticed. Luca reaches over and squeezes my hand. We are all panting and out of breath. The adrenaline is wearing off and I begin to shake. I realize that I haven't slept in what feels like days but the clock on the dash says we are just shy of five a.m.

"Are you kids all right? Anybody want to talk about it?" My dad inquires from the front seat and I can see he is stealing glances at me in his rearview mirror. He is worried but I just want to sleep.

I give him a nod and then add, "I will want to talk about it after I sleep for fifteen hours straight." He gives me a small smile in return.

I am so caught up in the moment that I forget we may be getting tailed. I turn to look over my shoulder to see if there are any headlights pursuing us but the street is black and empty as The Alliance fades from view. When I turn back around, Sasha is looking at me.

"Don't worry. There were measures taken so they couldn't follow us and more security measures have been put into place but we will catch you up to speed once we make it to our safe haven." She turns back around and I look to Luca. Through all the mayhem, I haven't been able to appreciate the fact that he is here next to me again. The hole I had felt in his absence is filled now and I feel whole again. He leans over and plants a kiss on my temple and I smile at the warmth of his lips on my skin.

"So? You really are the Romeo to my Juliet huh? Just without all the suicide and what not?" He smiles his easy smile at me, his eyes crinkling in the corners.

"How about I am the Edward to your Bella? That seems more fitting if you ask me." I laugh and lean into him, my head resting on his shoulder.

"So what now?" I ask but I don't stay awake long enough to hear the answer. I close my eyes and allow the tears to come. My mom is gone, lost to the dark side. I think I would've rather her been dead.

Chapter 14

When I awaken, I am on a cot in a place I don't know and I am all alone. There is an oil lamp burning next to me and I look around the room. It is large, no art on the walls, no windows, no other furnishings aside from the cots running down both sides of the room like a war hospital I have seen in old movies. My duffle bag is beside me and I am a little chilly. I see I am wearing a t-shirt and running shorts, so I slip my hoodie over my head and try looking for my phone so I can figure out what time it is or even what day it is. Where is everyone?

I don't remember anything since I fell asleep in my dad's car so I don't have a clue if we are even in North Carolina at this point. I am starting to feel afraid, claustrophobic even, but I look over at the cot to my right and see my copy of *Twilight* sitting at the foot of the bed so I know that Luca is here somewhere. When I look over at the cot to my left, I see my dad's travel bag with his initials embroidered on it… a Christmas gift my mom and I got him when I was in seventh grade and he was carrying all his toiletries to conferences in a Ziploc bag. We figured he was deserving of an upgrade. Thinking back on the memory makes my chest ache. The images of my mom rushing through my mind with her cold and hard eyes and her mocking smile. It was like she was a shell of her former self, completely hollow and empty on the inside. I shudder at the thought as I hear someone open a door.

My head spins to the right and I see Luca making his way

toward me, his own lantern in hand. When he gets close enough I can see the worry lines on his face. I feel so guilty. Ever since this boy met me, I have had him stressed out to the max and then to find that my mom is the root of all evil and he got dragged into this mess makes me feel even worse. I try to make light of the situation.

"How far back in time did we travel because I could swear that electricity had been invented when I fell asleep?" His mouth twitches in response to my comment as he takes a seat at the foot of my bed and we just stare at each other. I want to reach out and touch him but I also feel the need to commit all of him to memory. The way his nose slopes, the spray of freckles across his cheeks, the glacier blue of his eyes, his angular jaw and sharp cheekbones. Everything about him screams perfection and I know deep down that I feared he would look at me and see nothing short of average. I feared one day he would walk out and leave me too but after talking to Darcy and hearing about our chemistry, I know he is mine for the taking.

He leans forward and cups my face in his hand. I lean my face into his palm and then turn to kiss the inside of his wrist. When I look back to him, I can see the softness in his eyes that he saves only for me. He leans forward and our lips touch. My body feels like it will take flight with all the butterflies in my stomach and I just pray that this feeling stays forever. I know they say it wears off after a while but I don't think he will ever stop being so exciting to me. Each time I see him, every time I feel his touch, it is like he is a shiny new toy on Christmas day.

Our lips move together, slow and gentle. I don't even have time to process that I just woke up and probably have morning breath because he wraps his arms around my waist and tugs me onto his lap. I wrap my legs around his waist and take his face in my hands. The kiss becomes more urgent, deeper, as if it may be the last time we ever kiss. His hands trail up my spine under my shirt sending chills all over my body. I can hear water running overhead, the sound of forks scraping on plates in another room, whispers between Darcy and Demora off in the distance. I can smell soil, rich and fragrant and the moisture in the air can't be ignored. Luca's mouth is still moving firmly against mine with a hunger I haven't seen before and he has our bodies pressed so close together that I am finding it hard to breathe.

Finally, I pull away and see a tear is rolling down his face, his eyes still closed. I quickly use my thumb and wipe it away before taking his face in my hands again.

"Baby! Hey, open your eyes and look at me," I say to him gently, voice almost a whisper. The use of a pet name rolls off my tongue so naturally that it surprises me. When his eyes meet mine, I can feel myself melting into a puddle. "What is wrong?"

"I just – I love you, Gemma. I feel things I have never felt. When we are apart I feel an emptiness that is all consuming and I was so afraid. I was afraid when I was strapped to that chair that I wouldn't make it out or you wouldn't make it out of there or neither of us would. I knew before then that I loved you. But it was then that I knew I couldn't ever live a day without you. As you stood before me all brave and warrior like, I just knew that if anything happened to you, I would be lost." His voice is thick with emotion and I can't help but cry too.

"Luca, I love you too. You fill a void I didn't even know I had." He is looking up at me through his wet lashes, the vulnerability written on his face. "When you were taken, it was like part of me was missing. I love you so much." He breathes a sigh of relief like he was actually worried his feelings wouldn't be reciprocated. We sit there, foreheads pressed together, eyes closed, quietly crying. For me, it is a mixture of relief that he is okay, sadness about my mom, worry for our future, and what lies ahead for us. My arms looped around his neck, legs wrapped around his waist, and his arms wrapped around me, I realize there is someone standing at the foot of the bed, startling me and reminding me that we aren't the only two people in this world.

"I thought I might find the two of you together," Darcy says with a shy smile, arching one perfectly shaped eyebrow. I would have thought that as a mom, she would feel uncomfortable finding her son and his girlfriend in this position, but it seems to not affect her at all. "We are having a meeting. Everyone. In the dining hall. I'll give you two a few minutes." Then she leans down and wraps an arm around my shoulders giving me a small hug. Feeling a mother's love after the time I have had makes me want to burst into tears all over again. "I am so glad that you are okay," she whispers in my ear, "BOTH of you." She pinches Luca's cheek and turns for the exit. "And, Gemma... as dangerous as it was for you to go off on your own, thank you. Thank you for what you did. Putting your own safety at risk to save my son. We are lucky to have you." She closes the door behind her and we are alone again. As hard as I am finding it to keep my hands to myself, I know that we need to go so we don't keep the others waiting.

As we make our way out the door to head toward the dining hall, I realize the door opens into a dimly lit hallway. This room has lights but they barely illuminate the long hall. "Where are we?" I ask Luca as we walk down the hall toward a door on the opposite side.

"We are in The Alliance's underground bunker. It was built for emergency situations but we've never had one so it hasn't been used much." He has my hand in his and the other hand is holding a lantern.

"Well, I suppose that explains the lack of lights." I shudder to think we are underground and I suddenly feel extremely claustrophobic.

"Yeah. There are solar panels but they are for lighting the common areas like the dining hall, pathways, kitchen, and restrooms." As we near the door, I can see that this is a heavy-duty door. Luca unlocks it before holding it open for me to step through. We are in the dining hall and there has to be a minimum of fifty other people in here. My jaw drops as everyone takes their seats. The tables are long with chairs lining both sides, almost identical to the cafeteria back at The Alliance. Luca marches me toward the front of the center table where Darcy is already gearing up to address everyone.

As we walk forward, I pass my dad and Abigail. I release Luca's hand long enough to throw my arms around both of their shoulders and give them a brief hug, kissing my dad on the cheek, before moving to take my seat. Demora is standing with Darcy and gives me a small smile before whispering, "Welcome, my dear." Then Darcy is drawing all the attention to herself.

"Hello, everyone and welcome to the underground bunker. We were hoping the day wouldn't come when we would need this but here we are. I hope you will all settle in nicely because I am not entirely sure how long we will have to call this home." Murmurs break out around the room, everyone looking to each other, unsure of what that means. Darcy takes a brief pause before continuing, "It has been brought to our attention that the SGP's newest Vice President is none other than our own Genevieve Jacobs." More voices rise as the disturbing news spreads through the room. All these people that she has helped and then turned her back on feel betrayed. Out of the corner of my eye, I see Amy over in the corner throw her hands over her face, her shoulders shaking with sorrow. Again, I can't pity her as much as I normally would. I lost much more than she has. "The Alliance back home in North Carolina is no longer safe so we will remain here in Tennessee until it is safe to go back. In the meantime, thank you to Sasha for protecting our location. However, Sasha has some earth-shattering news that I would like for her to share with you." Darcy nods at Sasha and takes a seat next to Luca. As Sasha approaches the front of the room, there is a quiet murmur all around the room. The whispers and accusations are flying and nipping at her back as she takes a stance at the front of the room.

Sasha looks like death warmed over. Her hair is scraped back into a messy bun, her face free of make-up, an oversized t-shirt and sweats hide her thin frame, and bags under her eyes tell me she hasn't slept well in quite a while. She looks to me and Luca, takes a deep breath, and begins to speak.

"I betrayed you all. I especially betrayed you, Gemma. The package you received from the SGP wasn't left at the gate for you. It was personally handed to me to be delivered to you. I let the shield down so that they could approach our property and I allowed them to pass through to the other building." Luca's body goes tense next to me and heat radiates off of him. His anger is palpable. "I am so sorry but I have good reason and I promise they aren't excuses. As everyone knows, my mom Margo left me about a year ago never to be heard from or seen again. I thought she just disappeared much like Genevieve, but I was wrong. I was so wrong. Hughes and Adams showed me pictures of her in a jail cell." There is a gasp that shakes the room. Darcy has to stand now.

"Everyone. Please listen up! Let Sasha finish and then I will pick up where she leaves off." Darcy turns to Sasha, placing a hand on her shoulder and giving it a squeeze before she sits back down. Sasha takes a few breaths to calm her nerves and I look at her, really look at her. This is the girl to blame for everything we just went through yesterday or... crap. What day is it already? But I am not angry with her. I see the fear in her eyes, I know the desire to have her mother back. I have experienced that same yearning but I also now know why she has been acting so strangely since that package arrived.

"They have my mother, but they also have others. They promised to release her if I helped them retrieve Gemma but I couldn't... I couldn't exchange one person's freedom for another's. It isn't my place and, again, I am sorry to you all. Sorry that you had to leave The Alliance behind. Sorry that we are in this underground bunker until such time as to be determined. Sorry that I got us all into this mess by not coming to you, Darcy, or even you, Demora. You two have been wonderful to me and I failed you." She goes to walk away with tears streaking her face, but Demora stands and hugs her. I see the tension in Sasha's body literally ebb away as Demora uses her gift. I also feel more relaxed and at ease myself. An ability that some would think is so insignificant comes in handy more often than one would think. Darcy stands and moves back to the center of attention.

"The SGP is holding others in cells. We only know of Margo, but we are researching other members of The Alliance that we haven't heard from in a while. We assumed that so many had tried to blend in and lead normal lives, but I am afraid that may not be the case for some. The SGP was able to transport into places completely undetected. They were able to shield their presence. This is the work of talents we didn't know the SGP possessed. So there has to be more of us being held captive." Darcy clears her throat and locks eyes with Luca, an unspoken communication passing between the two of them.

"But," Darcy continues, "I have an announcement to make. Demora and I have decided that we can't lead this mission alone and have decided to appoint two new members to the board to aid with this. I am sure many of you have heard of the destinati amantes, or destined lovers. These two people together are stronger than any one single person. They feed off each other's talents making them practically unstoppable. Fortunately for us, we have our very own destinati amantes with us in this room. Luca, Gemma, would you mind standing?"

I feel all color leave my body. This is huge. Big. I have been a part of The Alliance for a whole five seconds and, after what my mom did, are they sure having another Jacobs on the board would be wise? Luca stands next to me but I just look up at him, mouth wide open. I don't do public speaking. I hate talking in front of crowds. Matter of fact, in eleventh grade speech class I threw up in a trash can in the front of the room before giving a speech on why college athletes should be paid. All of this running through my head as it feels like I am under water, drowning out the applause around me.

Luca reaches down and wraps a hand around my elbow before helping me to my feet but I just look around the room and quickly sit back down. Luca wraps an arm around my shoulders and pulls me into his side, my head against his hip.

"So, son, what do you say?" Darcy looks at him proudly while I am silently thanking her for addressing him and not me.

"I say we finally give those SGP sons of bitches what they deserve, what they've had coming to them for quite some time. Let's free our people." The room erupts in hoots and more applause.

Luca bends down planting a soft kiss on my lips and

whispering so only I can hear him. "Are you in, princess? You ready to fight like a Jedi with me? Be the Leia to my Han Solo? Ready to lead the rebellion?" I grab his face and pull him in for a long kiss, my cheeks flushing when I remember we are in a room surrounded by dozens of people.

"Your battles are my battles. Where you go, I go. Where you run, I run. I love you." Luca smiles his angelic smile, the smile that stole my heart, and kisses me again.

"I love you too, princess."

And that is how the war against my mother started.